Labor
of Love

Labor of Love

Keeping the Hope Alive

Linda Bridges

iUniverse

LABOR OF LOVE
KEEPING THE HOPE ALIVE

iUniverse books may be ordered through booksellers or by contacting:

iUniverse
1663 Liberty Drive
Bloomington, IN 47403
www.iuniverse.com
1-800-Authors (1-800-288-4677)

Because of the dynamic nature of the Internet, any web addresses or links contained in this book may have changed since publication and may no longer be valid. The views expressed in this work are solely those of the author and do not necessarily reflect the views of the publisher, and the publisher hereby disclaims any responsibility for them.

Any people depicted in stock imagery provided by Getty Images are models, and such images are being used for illustrative purposes only. Certain stock imagery © Getty Images.

ISBN: 978-1-5320-5210-1 (sc)
ISBN: 978-1-5320-5211-8 (e)

Library of Congress Control Number: 2018910955

Print information available on the last page.

iUniverse rev. date: 09/22/2018

Acknowledgment

I would like to express my thanks of gratitude to our Father. Who through the empowerment of His Spirit encourages me to write. To be bold and share the writing. Whom all praises and glory is given in this book in my Lord and Savior Jesus name.

I pray for all who read this book to be encourage in their hope and faith in the loving Word. I pray that you pray before reading this book to get past the enemy barriers to keep you from reading it for the wisdom inside. I encourage you to pray for a holy understanding. I rebuke and bind the spirit of fear, distraction, and laziness in Jesus name. I ask the Lord to instill in you His love, power, determination, and peace. Be bless.

I thank Him for many mentors in my life. Pastor Ary Ross, Lula M. Thames, Idella Knight, Elmer Campbell, Billy Ray Clark, Rose Clark, and family. Yes, so many others. Thank you for your encouragement, prayers, and listening ears. I thank IUniverse for their patience and nudging.

I searched for a way to keep my grandchildren enlightened by the Word. I began to call them and read to them bed times stories built on the Word. My intentions were to keep the hope alive. To keep them connected to the Lord in a way their minds would hold on too. I realize if I was having a challenging time keeping the Word flowing other parents or grandparents were too. The Spirit lead me to share.

Pray for me as I continue to pray for you.

I delicate this book to my grandchildren: Destiny, Daijhua, Devon, and my children Alaide, Joe, and Danielle whom have grows holy wisdom to bless me.

Agape (here and after) always in Jesus name.

KEEP THE HOPE ALIVE

We Labor In Love

I decided to write some of my daily activities on paper. They say it help to keep one's sanity. My relationship with Jesus help me with that. People do need to know what happening. They will wonder is this fact or fiction. I hope this help them to believe and keep the faith when horrors start to happen in real life. Our life is our greatest testimony, our greatest glory to God. If I get emotional forgive me, I am trying to keep my faith alive.

When I was young, I was raised on a small farm. We had an outhouse. Now I am telling my age. Time has changed and they have become strangely harder. I used to believe that the futuristic earth on television would come to pass. I thought that would be cool. I see the truth now. We will not have our cake and eat it too. I used to worry about life being left on this planet for my children. I don't have to worry now. Everything He prophesied is happening!

I had adorable children. They learn easy. They went through the potty training steps quickly. They did their homework and I checked it and all was good. Then one day I wondered whose children are these I'm raising. The change was sudden and unexpected. Later I had learned what happen.

Sometimes I have problems with getting the children to see the end times. To make it more difficult our communication got awkward and they became rebellious. I couldn't even recognize my own children. I remember they loved church as I did. They did beautiful drawing and colorings for me; I still have copies. We'd grin and talk about life. But now it's like I am talking a foreign language, I get ignored, they falsely accuse of getting in their business. We had that out. I ask what business, your life is an open book; literally an open book, you put everything on the internet.

I told them "I love you. I have your best interest at heart. I will find a way to pay for your financial education. I will back you up right or wrong. I will stand with you but you will reap what you have sowed."

I think this all started when I read her computer she forgotten she left on. Nothing new, I pick clothes up in her room she forgets a lot. I helped her clean it. Its like she needs nothing from me but food, clothes, shelter and money. Mainly to keep the cell phones on, they seem off more than on, due to the reception. They don't like me reminding them this will change. They are growing up. I remind them of my life insurance and to keep my burial simple. And I simply tell them I won't be here forever. But Jesus will. I told them we will always be together, we are family, but family in Christ first. We do not serve or bow down to images and we shall not receive chips or the marking in or on our bodies. I told them no tattoos or piercings but I found out later I was talking to the wall. Much to pray for. It true when they grow up they keep you on your knees praying. (Joshua 24:15). Yep, they remind me a lot about myself.

* * *

I used to be in the in crowd. I could walk the walk and talk the talk. I gave the world my all. I gave my heart so many times that when I came to the Lord it was shredded. I tried to pretend it was water under the bridge but my bridge had flooded long ago, overloaded from things I dump into it daily. Yea, you can say I was one of those that looked-for love in the wrong places. I decided as a teenager not to have children. The Lord change my heart, think to Jesus I did not end up in an abortion line. I truly can say somebody prayed for me.

Uh oh in the name of Jesus. Lord forgive me I did not intend to use your name in vain. What a day! Destruction in the land just like you said Lord. The government has actually taken and lost people's children. They say peace, peace and we have travailing in the land.

Since my eyes been open I have learned to trust no one, but Jesus. I am a cautious person but I walk around people more cautiously with good reasons. Then I heard a testimony of a Lady who said she was talking to a demon disguised as a human and he praised God as well as she did and wanted to keep in touch. The Holy Ghost reveal the truth to her. Now I know something, I just know some people are demon possess or is a demon.

✽ ✽ ✽

I went to a large common Supercenter Food Market the other day. I needed some odds and ends because I am storing up food, water, and comfort items as I can afford it and grab it. They have some useful info on how to start stocking on you tube. I must start somewhere and keep it up while I can, because you cannot trust the free help these days.

I need more frozen goods and lean meats. The cans are better some say but I want safe long storage so I use Mylar bags and oxygen absorber when I dehydrate my food. Also, glass jars for preserving last forever but take up a lot of space. I got my list and its going on Tuesday; the crowds should be small.

The people in the Supercenter are very disgruntled. Peace is a rare commodity if you do not have Jesus. The Prince of this air do not want peace on the job, no peace in the homes, no peace in the schools, and no peace when you sleep.

I see people scanning with chips in their hands like it is impressive. I think many people have not read their bible and better yet, they do not believe in their bible.

My source says that the militant will fill the street. And if you do have the chip they can track you or if you have a smart card you can still be tracked. There is nowhere to hide but in Jesus. The bible explicitly says do not receive the chip or a mark!

I finished shopping and managed to get in and out with no more than a strange look because I used cash. People steal your identity like they're standing right over your shoulder so I made sure no one is there or that the scanner is not copying my card. I use cash mostly. I have had people to approach me like I know them and try to start a controversial conversation. I murmur and keep walking. I absolutely do not want to bring the children out here. I fill up my tank looking relaxed, cocky, and a do not bother me attitude. It was a good day; I made it back home.

The mental trials and tribulations are bothersome on the jobs, in the schools, or in the churches; they are soul searching and challenging. I ask myself am I overcoming? If not time to repent and ask Jesus what is it, Lord? I do not want my work to be in vain. Because disobedience is as witchcraft. They, the disobedient or antichrist, are sitting in the churches building altars of destruction in the Lord's house. Some not knowing their hearts are not true, because their leader has told them all is well.

✽ ✽ ✽

Ministers that you have known for years come out of the closet or have outside children, they are stealing from the treasury (from God). You must go to the church with the whole armor of God and be ye ready because they are shooting and killing in the churches. We can't just talk about the Catholic churches they all got issues. Peoples beliefs and situations have taken a turn for the worst because the hope is dying. Sin is sin. Many believe that once you believe you are saved then you are always saved. These traps can be different, such as in following crowds, they tell you are always save, they tell if you repent for the same sin before you die you are forgiven, they tell you are a god, etc. You have been given the Lucifer complex. Will you be with the crowd? Are you in the box? Stay peculiar. I know a name can get blotted out of the book of life. Jesus takes unrepentance sins very serious. You for a fact get penalized by the world anyway so be on the winning side and remember stay away from the crowds.

There was a time I could do my work and go home, hopefully to peace. Good luck with that. (I know there no such thing as luck.) Another topic is broken homes. I know because I was raised in one. I have always tried to keep order and discipline in my home, blindly following Jesus did I achieve that.

God's children are associating with witchcraft, altars, and curses. And in their ignorance, they are already compromising in their jobs, church life and thus their soul are forfeited. The Lord will wake us up with grace and mercy. The enemies and their attacks are subtle but can be devastating even crippling to the self-esteem which lead to decreased integrity in life and on the job. We are so not ready, it was Job integrity that kept him from cursing God. The vessel becomes so focus on the attacks, unaware, they are no longer on the path of righteous or a vessel fit for the Lord's use. I am seeing more and more people with nonchalant attitudes on jobs, in schools, hospitals, attorney, and etc. or they have always been that way. They are burned out. Burned out from trying to deal with life on their own, they can do this, but they are ignorant due to the beat down that they are receiving in the spirit realm. I realized in my relationship with Jesus that I must stay completely under His blood (Ephesians 6 the whole armor). Praying daily for my family to be under the blood as Job offer sacrifices for his. I cannot let trials and tribulations get me down, because I must pray for my enemies, for my country, and for this world. Those whom do not realize everything they have dished out follow them home and to their families. God said I will visit curses to the third and fourth generation. We should not be wondering why our children are having it so hard. Much to pray for. It's the only way I can go out every day and accomplish what the Lord have sent me out to do and keep the faith alive. I realize the enemy resources are large, especially with the church in their ignorance, they are aiding him, but Jesus is larger and His resources have no end.

Trying to instruct a doubtful or double minded (lukewarm) person is difficult. It's not surprising to see these people becoming caught up with confusion, or dissention at work. This person is not a free spirit and not serving God. Where is the sincerity? The people that really want to work get brought down in the confusion or in the paper work that is designing to distract them. I know I've been there. The Lord taught me to stay focused on Him.

The mind is attacked with the influence of demonic thoughts or actions. If allowed it will destroy all that you believe in that is holy and just; and this is not just from demon but through people you trust and church people. Jesus can save us from that. Remember the world is going to hell in a handbasket, this disaster is inescapable, but there is Jesus.

Going through the same trials and tribulations and wondering "why me Lord." I ask the Lord that question many times when it seems I was going through the same trials. After obeying God, I received the victory in Jesus name. The Lord reveal to me the need for trials and tribulations. It is necessary to grow up physically and spiritually stronger in the Lord. It brings us closer to God and we learned to stay there. This has built my faith.

I thought I had the faith of a mustard seed and then some. I was being chastised until I saw the pride and stubbornness that I was proud of. I called out to the Lord and repented for the remission of my sins. However, that was just the tip of my problems, I later realize I had not the faith of a mustard seed. I was so caught up in myself, thank God for grace and mercy. After receiving repetitions in my life now I seek God more. Faith grew with works and works with faith. A light bulb came on and I humbled myself and did it Jesus' way with Jesus help. I was my own stumbling block.

Children go easy on your parents. You probably know more about what going on out there than they do. If you are not in the living word; you still know wishy washy when you see it. The public schools are full of lies. They have prepared you for military because the school are like the military camps. You probably learned how to walk on eggshells at school.

Military will teach you not to thinks for yourself. It will have desensitized you so you will do as instructed without an conscious. They will feed you food that make you feel full but lack major nutrients. You will not have the energy or will to resist but rather fall in their line of life. You will not think for yourself; you will be a drone.

My child told me that his teacher kept a bat in the classroom. I ask my child why a bat in the classroom. I was told it like this in this class; the teacher past out a test paper with grades on it. One of his classmate did not like his grade. He was tall and lanky built and he consider himself tough. He informs the teacher that his brother leads a gang. He also told her that they would not let him down. The teacher stops what she was doing and boldly pick up her bat. She told the boy they could come but right now she was ready for him. The boy shut up and set quietly in the classroom. She did not have problem out of that child in the classroom.

Now teachers are taking guns to schools.

The children must know it is possible to learn how to pray, trust in God and allow Him to lead you in Jesus name. You need the Lord's help. because there is no other way. What is the Lord's help? It is His Salvation! My children get quiet when talking about school. They hold good grades but it's a no zone for deep discussion. They don't talk much or they might say something they did not intend too. Once when I visited the school and prayed, it literally felt like I gain the attention of a presence. I prayed anyway in Jesus name pleading the blood of Jesus.

Last night I had a horrible dream about a moment in my past. I cancel that dream in the name of Jesus. I rebuked the dream. I rebuked the spirit of guilt in Jesus name. I've been redeemed by the blood of the Lamb. The dreams do not depress me as before. I prayed to Father God to destroy the soul ties in Jesus name. I had to do this sometime while fasting and praying. All that heartache that went under the bridge took pieces of me also. The hurt, the abuse, the scars, the rejection ripped me spiritually and physically. I had to repent and I had to forgive; I was put back together spiritually and physically. I was in these relationships with friends willingly and in my ignorance, I made agreements with the demons in these relationships, guilty by association.

I heard the Prophets say they have seem people spirit man as a toddler in a corner bent down not moving. Caught in that horrific moment that they ran away from in real life. The enemy used that moment to entrap them. In real life this person could not remember very well, they had trouble making decisions, and easily influence, but the Lord delivered many of them. The Lord was able to reach way down and save the brethren, Jesus works like that; he doesn't stop until we are whole.

Remember every time you sin you open a doorway for demons to come in. I I wrestled not against flesh and blood, but spiritual wickedness. I realized I could not forget about them my sins, and picked up my life and went on as if nothing happened. I could not get rid of sin that way. I had to repent. I rebuked and cast out demons that was in my life and my family's life. I commanded them (the demons) to brings all parts of me back in Jesus name. I also prayed to Father God to send Holy fire to destroy altars made by my ancestors or family members; not only did they sell me out but they sold out their bloodline too. I am in their bloodline. I prayed to the Lord to destroy generation curses in Jesus name. This is faith. It's deep, and the battle is just beginning. In truth the battle is not ours it is the Lord. Going to hell should not be an option. Keep the faith. Sleep with your audio bible on at night very low to feed and strengthen your spiritual man, the real you. This works. The truth does set you free. (Hebrew 2:13)

The battle is just beginning because the mind must become free from satanic attacks. Cravings and addictions coming from the flesh that you are not aware of must be purged out. The spiritual man has been established, but the body may not yet be whole. Only Jesus knows and will make you whole. You could be one of those miraculous persons that surrender all and you are fully delivered and set free. Free from altars, curses, addictions, and shackles known and unknowns. You come out running for your life; you are running for Jesus. You are like the Cainite woman at Jesus' table begging for a crumb but you do have the faith, so your crumb turn into a loaf. Unfortunately, many of us have to grow that faith.

❋ ❋ ❋

I consider myself a smart person but I have been humble through trials and tribulations, but the Lord is not through with me yet. I thought the Lord had a sense of humor. He does, but was serious when he told me when you think you know something, you know nothing. Now I see that unfolding around me daily. Woe to those that are not walking in the true Light.

I was driving from work one morning. I was in a blessed mood. Praise music was blasting and I knew I was not alone in my van. Heavenly angels were singing with me and I cannot describe my voice its was at its peak that morning. I was feeling great. I heard a BOOM! I instantly lost control of the van. The vehicles behind me drop back while I was wobbling and trying to control the van. I immediately call out to the Lord. (Let me go back a month. The Lord told me I spend more money on my shoes than my tires. I ignorantly put it off thinking God is trying to tell me something. My God had a sense of humor. I brought that used rotted tire anyway.) I did a figure eight on the interstate. I knew I was going to flip. I prayed Lord if you do not help me I won't make it. The Lord instantly took control of the van. Yes, there was a strip of gravel then a deep ditch on the side of the road. In the Lord's hand the van slid side ward on the other side of the gravel and came to an instant stop. No one but God. I have since learned to take God sense of humor seriously.

Not only did he save me from the blow out but he sent a young man to change the tire. The young man would not take a penny although he needed the money. Needlessly to say I send many prayers to him till this day when I remember that man. God bless him and his family and meet their needs.

He did it again for me when I hydroplaned off the road. I knew I was a goner and called on the Lord in prayer. I would not let fear overwhelm me, it was there in plenty. When I went off the road, I closed my eyes, took my hand off the wheel and when I hear a voice say hit your brakes, I hit the brakes. We all have our miraculous testimonies.

I learn never to leave home without the Lord. Pray in my sleep as needed. I tell the Lord I accept all His dream and vision in Jesus name. I cancel all dreams and visions that not of you, Jesus, in Jesus name. I learn not to leave them hanging in the air or in the spiritual realm. Just because I have awakened and may forget the dream does not mean the enemy has. I do not allow the enemy to have his way with my destiny in the spiritual realm anymore, causing destruction, obstacle (hardships), pain, illness, grief, open can of worms, and the list could go on. This way I do not accept anything tricky or subtly implanted by the enemy. Otherwise the enemy continues to sow tares with the wheat and he steal your blessings. This way it is destroy (the stealth, the traps) before it takes root.

I watch a video of children while playing and kicking a child to death. They are desensitized to what they were doing. I pray for the minds of the children all over the world. Prayers for those enslave and a prayer for all the government systems. Lord we need help. Instead of watching soap operas people are watching the Whitehouse, the drama is ongoing. I was guilty, watching those soaps night and day, but the Lord revealed to me how it rots the minds. I made a vow to the Lord and I am not taking it back. I am not watching soap opera now, and television is not safe, hold onto the word because you may have to snap the TV off. The alternative is not acceptable. I hope now you have a picture of how my days are going now in the end of the end days. I know my Redeemer lives! I know he is coming back!

It is voting time again. I know people say we should do something. We should vote for varies reasons. Well I do believe one person makes a different because the Lord told us the prayers of the righteous availed much. But I do not see a different in the government systems. I keep the faith because I read the Book. I'd rather sign a paper which doesn't seem to matter, because it been proven that cheating in the government is real. I do not want to imagine what our government is being use for, since America is being called Babylon. And Babylon will be utterly destroyed, right now its location is Iraq.

I will continue to do my part, vote and pray. Until the stuff hit the fan, it's like paying taxes; I do not agree to what it's being use for but I trust Jesus. I render to Caesar that which is Caesar. In these day and times please pay tithes.

I had a discussion with a sister in the Lord yesterday, she was complaining about prayer being out of the school. She said more people should have sign the petition. I told her I believe they did but it did not reach the Whitehouse. We are in the end times and things will get worst. I said we should up our teaching of the bibles in our homes and the church. I told her it starts in the homes sister.

There's been some bombing with meteorite showered, we are not sure. Whatever they say and we take it with a grain of salt. Dormant volcanoes going off. They tell us all is well, will be well, and everything under control. In our arrogance and ignorance, there was a time we believed them, the governments and the churches. Through dreams and visions, we found the truths (Amos 3:7). We know what is causing the fires and why more people are disappearing every day. There is an underground news that some nations have stopped using paper money; the chip is now mandatory. They must use chips for everything. Many have refuse and they are suffering, to God be the glory there are those that are staying steadfast in the Lord. The Lord had warned us. We that trust the Lord knew the truth. Nothing in the history books or news can be trusted or prepare us for what to come but Jesus.

We cannot predict the weather for evidence point to the government controlling it. God's word is true, prophecies are being fulfill. People are watching nature's fury from their back yards. Hawaii is one nation. People wake up to volcanoes spewing and erupting lava in their backyard and neighborhood, sink holes in their yard, people are never found because their house have fallen in. Warning before destruction; be ye ready. Dreams and visions have prophesized New York devastation. Now even the scientist agrees it just a matter of time. They believed it have happened before. New Orleans is very much aware of their upcoming predicament. It was prophesied, even the scientist's research give evidence that coastland and more will go underwater. My prayers and heart goes out to my brethren be ye ready. Keep me in your prayers as I keep you in mine. Father God whom we serve is the same past, present, now, and future in Jesus name. He will not forsake us. Yes, it will only get worst. No rock will be left unturned. We are only safe in Jesus.

The Bible is truth. It showed us history repeating itself. God will destroy nations that have become abomination and our country at the top. You cannot mock God on a global level and not expect correction. Fear God!

He could wipe out our bloodline. Be thankful God stopped at us, and that because of his Son's blood and we repented sincerely.

Be thankful, if your body is deadly ill but it recovers because of his Son. He could allow the enemy to leave you covered in boils or strike your bloodline with crippling diseases that amaze the doctors. Yet your body linger in agony. They will invent new name for something that already been here. (There is nothing new under the sun). And the medicine they get to invent and try out will probably be use in warfare or had been used in warfare.

Be thankful, if any of us is caught up in the rapture it will itself be a miracle. Our minds have been in a comfort zone for a long time, can we image a nation undergoing what Job in the bible went throughs. What Egypt went throughs. It happened. That the tip of our Father God brief history dealing with us, a rebellious, backsliding, and adulterous people. He could allow the smallest country in this world to defeat us. This has been done. Bottom-line is this country will be humble. Every knee will bow and every tongue will confess His Son, Jesus Christ, Yahshua (Hebrew name of Jesus), is Lord.

And for those that falsely see Satan, as god, will see scriptures after scriptures fulfilled. You are still breathing so you too can repent and be saved. You will know when the scripture says he will be drag to the lake of fire in chain. Where he is so will be his followers.

Oh my! Another earthquake in California, I am grateful that it stopped. I did not know if this would be the one. The one that even scientist say will take California off the map. No place is safe. Earthquakes are pass our understanding, tsunamis, storms, and pestilence we do not have a name for them we cannot predict accurately. The ground does not want to grow food no matter what you do to pump it up. I know the Bible is being fulfilled.

They increase martial law. They said because of "terrorist's attack", I've known it a matter of times before they'd announce the one-world government. Lots of people are not concern except now they want complete control of the guns, and was confiscating the bibles. Taking those guns have really stir up the people; without Jesus there is no safety. They were more concern gathering the bibles than the guns. They realize without Jesus there is no hope. One day at a time sweet Jesus becoming my motto.

Abortion is used as a form of birth control. If it was not for truth, we would not have many children on the earth at this time. Free abortions have relieved many women and men of their responsibilities. I pray and watch because I learn worrying change nothing.

My sanity is on the edge. I am trying to save myself from this untoward generation. I'm trying to work out my soul salvation. I'm trying to raise God-fearing children.

I know now why children caved in so quickly. Why they love confusion but slow to do what right unless motivate. Do not want to learn how to drive, think college will wait forever, slow to leave home, and other things; where we were self-motivated.

I had seemed children instead of dealing with the problem just stopped eating, and started hanging out with a tough crowd. Especially when electronic went haywire. Like that would make it better. I let her know there are consequence to each type of actions. They do so many things wrong. I can see myself.

I gained information from my source about vaccine shots, flu shots, the air, ground, food, and so many other things that have damage us and our children. I bought and made appointments for my children to get most of these things. It has condition and desensitize my children. I did not spare the rod, I did not abuse them but I hope I kept them focus. I planted the word in them and pray I gave God something to work with.

The children know things are tense. I have talk to them about what's going to happen and where we stand. It not easy but they will know whose child they are. They will know the Spirit we serve. I told them we are family and we can always be together. I love my children. Bottom line we stand for Jesus because he stands for us. The image and the mark of the beast is unacceptable; we do not receive it. We will be together in heaven. Then they look at me cross way with their games and such. I told them evil does come across the music, friends, games, and so many things. It's so hard to compete with electronics.

I am praying as steadfast for others and myself. Face down praying. I was encouraged to get coffee today and met him. Praise God. It's embarrassing to say, but I am scared to go out these days. I am about to finish this with him, the prayer of salvation. I met him in the coffee shop. I rarely treat myself these days. But the Spirit lead and I follow. This man is desperate for a confirmation to his salvation and hungry for the word. Thank the Lord for sending me in here and he did not break down to a stranger. We go to the back of the building. We talk about the Lord. What draw him to Christ. I let him know I understood. I tell him to repeat after me. Father forgive me for I am a sinner. I repent for the remission of my sin in Jesus name. Jesus, I want you to become my Lord. Come into my life and my heart. I believe you died for me and shed your Blood on the cross for my sins. Be my personal Savior in Jesus name. Amen. Sir keeps the faith. Trust the Lord and lived your life by the word of God. Be ready. (We part.)

I went from a hard life to an easy life and back to a hard life. I cannot complain, it is true there is always someone or something worse. Many of the things we are doing does not seem strange to me. My siblings use to laugh at me for being conservative. Now look whose smiling.

It because it's paying off. My parents told me about these times and I heard about them in the Church too. Hard times are coming they said. It is more of a mental battle than physical. Got to keep the hope alive because the spiritual battle is real. Just ask yourself when all hope is gone will you still hold on? If you got faith in Jesus then the answer is yes. This is what it is coming down too.

❋ ❋ ❋

I pass places they were giving out free phones. Last week it was food. Lobbying for better health care packages with good deals. They give and they take it back. It sounds too good to be true. First you charge me an arm and a leg for health care now you want me to have it free. Sound too good to be true. I would hang around to see will these people come out or what will come out. I don't want to get caught up in the crowd. Avoid crowds, I believe there is body snatchers out here. It dangerous out here.

The battle does begin in the mind. Even when I am sleeping I'm fighting. The Lord taught me how vulnerable my spiritual man can be. The battle continues even when we sleep. The Spirit taught me how to reinforce the whole armor of God on my spiritual man. How to truly gridle up. Because the real me is the spiritual man. I have started playing the bible on low volume at night while I am asleep, even around y children as they sleep The more understanding of the spiritual battle, the stronger your armor (Ephesians 6). You know how we say a little prayer a little power. A lot of prayer a lot of power. It like that.

Just when I think it has cooled down, more confusion pops up in the land. Satan knows his season is short, we underestimate how desperate he is. Things are becoming worst because now it is closer to our homes. We thought staying in the country would help, it did for a short while. There no place but in Jesus to be safe. We must not let fear destroy us. Fear causes the mind to freeze, it sets you up for destruction without a fight. It sets you up to leave a spiritual door open to the kingdom of darkness, don't lose hope stay gridled up in the living word.

The schools are scary. The children do not want to go or ride the bus. They complain about perverse things going on in the school and on the buses. They say the adults turn a blind eye. The children were scared and the parents did not force them to go. I was impressed with their next step.

The children want to go to school now. I smile at that. I remember a time they would hope school would be close. They always desire more days off. They do not go to a school building. They go to school at a Christian house where we also attended church. There they also meet other children. They know the rules, always rules now and they must be careful. The schools are not far. It was kind of the lady to include our children in her home schooling.

I get most of my information from Christian homes where we have church. Some manage to keep their jobs. They try not to bring attention to themselves, they know there's only a matter of time. They stay below the radar. I mean they live in this world but not a part of it, spiritually speaking, I do too.

Church attendance is not what it was cracks up to be. They used to say come as you are back then; they meant come in your Sunday best. Now you really go as you are. The building does not look like a church. I think I said it earlier, I must be careful. You know Spirit filled church members when you meet them. The Spirit of the Lord will not allow me to be deceived or ignorant.

I must be alert sober and vigilant, keeping the faith. They are removing us. Sometimes whole families go missing. If the Holy Spirit does not acknowledge them I keep stepping. Must stay on point, obedience is essential. It is painful to see families against families. Those houses they left alone.

We try to stay close together, when some people come back they are changed. We pray and the Lord reveals they have indeed submitted (bowed to the enemy). They did not receive the mark of the beast or the chip yet but there are other ways to bow to the beast's image. We pray and the fear is removed. There are people in pain and hearing voices and found out they have been chip; they do not know what to do. The government knows and ignore them. I cannot let fear overcome me must be ready to move. Some do and do not come back.

I wonder and ask how a strong educated person break down to the lies. A sister explained to me. She said, "they are weakening those in the spiritual realm, because the spiritual man has not been feed the word of God. That is, it strength and food," "we have the power of the Holy Ghost and seek God daily", she said, "the word lives in us; not just lip service." Then she said something very interesting that even I could relate to with my fatigue and lack of drive. Sister said, "We are attacked at a cellular molecular level in our DNA by our lack of nourishment from our food and radio waves designed to attack molecules we need to keep our body strong." She later told me this is through cellular waves of cell phones, towers, routers, smart meter, and many other things in our house. We don't stand a chance without Jesus, who makes us whole.

I never thought to be here in these times. If anyone ask me I would just smile and walk on. I'm hoping and kept praying to escape this tribulation. At that time, I thought God would not let this happen to us. Even though I knew one day it would happen. It was a reality check.

We thought the Great Deception was going to happen in the end days. It's already afoot. Many are still sleeping, waiting on the Big Deception with signs. Because the Lord revealed to me the Great Deception began when Satan stole Adam and Eve blessings. He began to change this world to cause us to fail. He stirred up a lust so strong that he caused the angels (watchers) to sleep with the daughters of men. We do not stand a chance without Jesus. We are weak but Jesus is strong, and Jesus is our advocate.

The Deception is afoot and we have been deceived and living a life of vanity and lies. Jesus' truth set us free. It gives new meaning to lean not toward my own understanding but in all things, I acknowledge Him, the Lord, and He will direct my path. It's an eye opening experience to realize the world is a lie and an illusion wrapped up in a blanket of confusion. Thank Father God there is hope in Truth. Because truth follows peace and peace follow truth. The Truth do indeed set us free.

Mother against daughter, father against son. We have homes nursing children from shock. They were promised freedom, food, shelter, and electronic, and such. Thank God many was not ready to leave their family. Many, through prayer, have been awakened. When their laptops, tablets, games, and especially cell phones shut down, they clamp up. We notice children have stop eating. They look and acted like zombies. I know they could betray me but they are my children, I will still keep the faith.

The children were zonked out and attack anyone feeling with hurting words. You felt like you've been chewed- up and spit out. We prayed for many and they were set free in the name of Jesus. Some we had to exorcise to complete their deliverance. I notice if the word was planted in them there was something in them to set free in the name of Jesus.

Some was not so fortunate to be set free. As soon as they could they ran away and did everything the government told them to do. We had to separate ourselves. Oh, the pain families felt from losing love ones. They turn toward the church family and embrace them more.

❋ ❋ ❋

I am still accepting what is unfolding before me. Then a new reality came forth, more church members were not what they appeared to be in the Lord. They did everything in the church according to rules and traditions, but was lacking. We tried to talk to them but they were set in their ways. We knew a separation was happening. The bible fulfills, you will know them by the fruit they bare. They just walk away, no resistance, lead like sheep to the slaughter. "If they are mine my power (my anointing) will follow them" said the Lord. We know what He meant when He said the very elect will barely be saved. All I have is faith, hope in Christ Jesus, the alternative is not acceptable. Mercy Lord. I know the Holy Ghost will not let me be deceived.

Fear in the land have confused and frozen many. Fear is one of our worst enemies. It causes many to give up without questioning or resisting. Us that are wisely saved stand on the Rock. Our salvation is upon the Rock. We know in Christ we are not given the spirit of fear but of power, love, and a sound mind. We resist and trust no man. Trust only Jesus. (Matthew 12:21)

Those I thought many around us was rooted in the living word, but I am given giving an awakening. They gave up their faith. Then they gave up those that trusted them. Such deceit. They even justified it as being the will of God. They tried to make us think we made a mistake. They mix truth with lies and that deceive many. It was what their itching ears wanted to hear. Half-truths which there are no such thing, simply put are lies. I know there can be no lukewarm, no straddling the fence, or gray areas. We stride to be ready. In these times the line is drawn, sheep are being separated from the goats. We know now they wanted us to blaspheme. They knew what they wanted. We knew what we wanted. When they came back many were gone.

This made me think of Stephen in the bible. First, they rally for him. He was highly recommended as a man of God. Then they wanted him stones from lies their itchy ears wanted to hear (Acts 7:59). Yet he forgave them and stayed true to his path with faith in tack. The only way we all should go; will I be ready?

There will be some not dead when my Lord comes back; I know the rapture is upon us. The Lord told me "do not get left behind and pray to escape the tribulations that coming upon the world." (Luke 21:36). Be ye ready. Now I see the living word unfolding before my eyes every day. How foolish and selfish I was. I now have eyes to see, now I see the earth rejecting us. This earth that was supposed to be cherished.

When bodies die, they use to be simply prepared and given back to the earth. Now they are selfishly prepared as if the body should last forever and they are treated and then fitted to poisons the earth. This body is temporary not meant to last forever like our spiritual man.

The bible told me we come from dirt and dirt we will go back too. This body is on loan to us. It is temporary. God's plan is for us to change from mortality to immortality and corruptible to incorruptible. Then we will be as the angels. The earth is the stop over or preparation place. This body will not go with me; it will return to the earth. The body takes some wear and tear as we decide where to spend eternity and some are still choosing wrong. The wear and tear we put on God's body; the things we make it do will bring us to a day of reckoning with an angry God. Grace and mercy Lord.

So many have taken the mark and have encouraged their friends and family. Schools, churches, hospitals, government officials, and some jobs are making it mandatory. They falsely think they will live forever.

Water in abundance and none to drink the Lord warned me about this day. I tried to get a private well but the government had control even back then. They've started off with yes, we will dig you a well; then gave me reasons why they could not.

Land to plant food but unable to grow it. Those that have food do not always share. Yes, we are in for rough time. We girdle up and keep our integrity. We keep the faith believing the Lord have a ram in the bush for us and pray.

Horrifying actions from our government are spilling down to the people. Finding out most of our country is owned by outside nations, people hate us just because we are American. According to some doctors they believe we are very ignorant and easily influenced by things that would be of minor significance in a more intelligent group." Now we can clearly see there is no respect of person. We do not agree and trusted them so I am called ignorant. They see all of us like this now, they are genociding all people, I got to read up on Agenda 21 (google it). This is still on the governments to do list. They experiment with syphilis on people, diverse types of cancer as well and falsely diagnosing people have been going on for a while. Now it is believing that HIV, swine flu, the rise of autisms and many other health problems are caused by the enemy. Which means they are intentional. All types of people were experimented on with LSD, mustard gas, electroshock therapy to control the mind and it seemed to work. Chem trials, negative electromagnet waves and things we cannot imagine destroying our cells at a molecular level are quite effective. They have removed trace elements out of the foods, it gave us our basic building blocks for our cells regeneration; we see the results of that at work. But it has not gotten pass Jesus. The enemy has no respect of person. They've tried to hide the truth but it slips out. The Lord only knows it all. They been trying to control the mind for a while. I think they've gotten it right with the music, TV, churches, chip, and drugs. Fortunately, our mind is not controlled by spirits, chips, and drugs only Jesus who keeps us whole.

It still amazes me. When people (church people) not rooted in faith change before my eyes. People on the street and sinner are not coming in for help; they are afraid. The street people trying to tell the news cast what's happening. It's not good news, the reporter stopped recording. They did not follow up. People continue to disappear. I cannot believe what I see on TV no matter how big the story.

We are still ministering and praying the prayer of faith with sinners; you must be led by the Spirit. The sinner seems to grasp what was happening before the church people. They say if the head is sick so will be the tail. The world is sin sick. Our leaders have been passive in the country but active with the enemy. We now see the truth in that. As a minister stated the leaders preached a gospel of accommodations and not Jesus and this satisfy the massive. We in for more of a rough ride.

The Lord told me that's a Jezebel spirit is in the church, always ending in stirring up the lust of the flesh. I know the flesh does not need much help with that. It is in His church deceiving many and made many wants to be deceived. Those of little faith. Lord has mercy on us. Let it start with me. (Rev 2:20). I lived a fast life with crowds, the world seemed to be at my fingertips; I was so miserable. I had to let it all go. I had too when the Lord showed me the alternated.

The Lord revealed to me that many falsely believe they have the faith of a mustard seed. Really, they have no faith. So many are like the little rich ruler, who could not sell all he had and follow Jesus. We have instant gratification of water, food, clothes, entertainments, children (daycare center to care for them), and so many other things. The enemy uses this against us. It's easy to say I love you Lord and everything is at our fingertips; our heart is not there.

Now, I understand the word that God can only be served in spirit and truth. Without the Holy Spirit it's useless if I cannot have the faith of a mustard seed; I need it to decrease my flesh daily while walking this earth.

They say, "I am preparing to refuse, reject the mark of the beast." I am saying the same. They say with conviction and good intention, "I will not take on the image of the beast" but they are already sold out. The world aims to walk into this curse. To lead our children into this curse. We are born in sin and shaped in iniquity. The outer appearance looks holy but the inside is filthy. As Jesus said many time we are a generation of vipers.

The only reason I know I have a true conviction is by the power of Holy Ghost. I know it has its hands full with just me. I am barely holding on. Jesus is the way.

The Lord told me in the past that this world is an illusion. Nothing is as it seems. Lean not on your own understanding but trust Him in all things.

We are a people full of unknown addictions such as our food and is not aware of it. The food we eat is more addicted than the drugs on the street. It was late knowledge but they are cocky about letting us know what's going on, because they know we cannot do anything about it. Without Jesus, I can be caught up in their reality. It will control my emotions thus my mind to get me angry, happy, confuse, sad, and so many other feeling. Then my mind is off the time at hand. I can miss the rapture. Time to pray.

The enemy did a decent job; he can make you think you are doing right when it is clearly wrong. The discipline Paul stated, "when I would do good, evil is present with me." It looks, taste, feel good to do it. That deceived me at one time. I was like a sheep lead to the slaughter. A little sin or a little white lie will not send us to hell (another false belief). Many still believe this, I grab on to this belief when I was coming out of my mess. The truth set me free. I was falsely believing God is a God of love surely, he would not punish me forever.

The Great Deception will not be the time of the mark of the beast. Because it is already here. It was started with the four blessings he stole. Which are to be fruitful and multiply, subdue and replenish the earth, and have dominion over every living them. He is prince of this air for now.

We cannot send a roving accusing eye at Adam and Eve because we have done far worst. We cannot point an accusing finger at our ancestors. I see family not enforcing the Word in their children's life. The children are being sold out, no better than our ancestors did to us. Jesus is the way.

We cannot even reason with God as Abraham did to spare Lot. Because we have bypassed the sins of Sodom and Gomorrah. Thank Jesus for grace and mercy. Thank Jesus for the cross. Thank Jesus for his blood. We can repent with a sincere heart. We can be washed by His blood. We can bare our cross. We don't deserve it but his grace and mercy allows it. Who has not sin? Jesus.

The children are rarely sick, thank God. We cannot go to any doctors anyway. They want answers to too many questions, and have strict requirements. There are some Christian members that know a lot about herbs. I remember a few from my Mom and from trying to live healthy. The herb lady also gave me good recipes. I have on hand elderberry syrup, can watermelon rinds, blackberry root, pot root, milk thistle, and many others. We try not to waste anything. We are seriously trying to live off the grid independently.

Living off the grid is almost impossible, but with God all things are possible. We do try to live off the land with God's blessings, it's hard. The enemy has poisoned the land, poisoned the air, poisoned the water, poisoned the wild life. Truly we eat and drink deadly things and they do not harm us. The farms are under their control. They have taken control over private wells. We do not tempt the Lord our God we pray to stay true.

I sometimes envy the Amish life, they have not left much of their roots behind. They do not have to struggle to sustain. We on the other hand must backtrack and remember many simple survival techniques. I was raised on a farm and this reminds me of my roots. I thought life was hard. It goes to show how little I knew.

I have met a few herbalists that are resisting the changes. They're strongly believe in natural ways of living and being in touch with Mother Earth and their freedom. The want to live below the radar until things get better. As I said many times we know the truth, it will not get better but worst. They still need Jesus on their side. Remember I said the Lord reveal no lukewarm. We must believe and trust in Him only. Jesus is coming back. It's the only way to survive. Do you trust Jesus?

People are still disappearing. Big stores are shutting down for no reason. There rumors that they are becoming concentration camps. We're at war. But with who.? Now we know from our own country. People are disappearing.

I wore a dress to church the other day. I patched it together from old material. It did not matter. I felt so welcomed at this church building. We are always truly glad to see each other. We did not know whether we will meet on this side of the earth again or where. But we hope and prayed that we all cross the Jordan River to Zion when we do leave.

We don't care whether or not we can have guns any more. We do not care about social status, and we stopped caring if you are black, white, or any nationality. We stop caring about who gets to what bathroom.

Denomination is a thing of the past. We have a common denominator and that is God. We recognize Jesus as being his Son and our Lord. We clean to that truth. We are glad to believe.

Some of us are forced to hide from their persistence. All of us are waiting, not knowing when and where to flee, but we will be obeying God. We are in the countries, cities, houseboats, and mountains. We are affected by the changes.

They remove prayer out of school a long time ago and children started slaughtering themselves in schools. They don't want children to know if they are a boy or girl, a gender thing. They started giving out free cell phones. I knew those were bugged just like the others. The air is poison to us I'm told or should I say by negative electrode magnetic waves intentionally put in the air. There is nowhere to run or hide, float, but in Jesus. Where the Lord takes us, we'll follow. There are those of use that have eyes to see and ears to hear, we know what's coming.

There are the dreams and vision from God's interpretations. The enemies cannot take them away from us. We would be lost without the dreams. Dreams from the Lord as in the book of Joel that keep our hope alive. But many in their ignorance have forsaken their dreams. They compare them and seek understanding from manmade books. They do not seek God. They find them amusing as watching a television show. They go to church but they do know the God they serve. The Holy Spirit stirs within us. We must seek Him while He can be found. We know that time is near. Exactly when we do not know, but judgement is here. We pray to be ready. He is coming back.

Three Peculiar Pigs

Once there were three peculiar pigs. The first pig had hope. The next pig had faith. Our third pig had charity. The sweet little pigs left home and lost their adolescent. They grew up usually making few wrong choices, but that's getting ahead of the story. Do you want to know how? Each one started to grow and they began to make lazy decisions.

They had a Mom who was strict as tar. Once a rule was set it was unmovable. She knew her children were anointed and the enemy tried from their youth to destroy them. "God forbid", thought Mom. She was not going to have any of that.

The first two piglets were birthed with ease. The third little piglet came into the world a challenge. The birthing resembles what was in the land, confusion. It was a difficult birth. But with the family, friends, and prayer support, Mom and baby piglet were fine. Dad and Mom knew what they were getting into. They wanted babies. They wanted little kids to take up where they left off. They were prayer warriors and felt they had a lot to pass down. They felt it was there calling to be parents, that's what parents was for. They love their piglets. There were some rough spots but hope kept them going. There were some stones but faith kept them moving, and there were multitudes of faults but love covers them all. They made it through the changes of adolescence. They had managed to keep laughter, joy, chores, and communication in the home.

Changes come and they can be good or bad, but in the Word, we change not. Some outside families began to change when the Big Bad Shepherd entered the town. He immediately started throwing money around. Many brethren were impressed and left the fold. Many sold out and changed their behavior to blend in with the worldly crowd. They even took the time to entice their friends to give and participate. They should have known he was spending their own money on them.

The people of the town were a little confused at first but the people of the town held out. The people of the town knew the way they walked was not in vain. The people of the town did not bring the confusion in their home. The people that kept the faith separate themselves and kept the faith. They knew in the Spirit something was wrong.

The grass looked to green to be real. The enemy can only hide it true nature for a while. The relative started coming up missing. Flyers for missing pigs were popping up all over town. The cousins little and big pigs came up missing. The people of the town used to stay in the place where you did not have to lock your doors. Everybody knew almost everybody. Now no one knew who to trust. The people of the town trust Jesus.

The Big Bad Shepherd who turns out to be a Big Bad Wolf learned the activity of the town. He realizes all he had to do was buy lunch, compliment, and praise them. And their tongues rolls; they told everything. He knew the who's and the what's. It was finally proven what he was doing when bones were found in his home. What he did he had no shame. He did not try to hide them.

The piglets of the small town had invited the Big Bad Wolf over for meals. Later they turn out to be the meals. From the weight, he put on he was a glutton.

Many families went into hiding, lock up their doors, and repent. There were some of us that stood together. The people that did not fall for the Big Bad Wolf false teaching and tricks. The people that held steadfast to our Father's teaching. This part of the town did not bulge. We band together, and prayed.

So, when that Big Bad Wolf came before us and said, "I want to come in." The people that kept the faith did not tremble in fear. They said firmly, "NO"! Then he stated, I will settle for a one-time snack." The people that kept the faith said more firmly, "NO"! Then the wolf stated, "Then I will huff, and I'll puff, and I will blow your house in." The wind began to rage. The house rattles. The Elders replied (some being terrified but all kept the faith), "Matthew 8:26." They remember this scripture and spoke to the wind. "Why are ye fear, O ye little faith? Then he arose and rebuked the winds and the sea; and there was a great calm." They remember the Lord control the winds. They spoke to the wind be calm in Jesus name. The wind calms. The Big Bad Wolf tried to stir up more wind and more mess. It did not work. He froze in fear. He did not understand what was happening. He realized it was not working. What he did earlier at the other houses did not work here. He felt shamed, humiliated, and discredited. He was not as big or as bad as he thought. There was someone Bigger. The wolf walked off with his tail between his legs. Instead of learning his lesson the wolf soon began to plot his next meal. The wolf allowed himself to go to sleep with anger on his mind. The seed was planted. The wolf arose with vengeance in his heart and left the town.

He murmurs, "an eye for an eye, a tooth for a tooth and that's just the beginning, I will settle this score one day." With this thought in the wolf's mind he felt justified in lying, killing, and destroying lives. He realizes his luck was gone in this town; it was time to move on. And he did.

That was a night to be remembered and a story to be told for generation to come. And so, the three piglets grew up in a more peaceful time.

Those of us who have grown up we know eventually we leave home. Oh yes. The grown up needs their own home. It was time for the not so little pigs to leave home. The parents set the pigs off. They knew they would be challenged. They would do well if they do not let their stomachs get the better of them, and remember their daily prayers. They know if they work they will eat, and to eat you must work.

Off they went down the road. The eldest pig stomach started growling. He murmurs, "when it was just me at home I ate all I wanted." That was before his brothers came along. He looks at his brothers and gave them a sweet smile. First pig said, "I know farmers in this area. It looked prosperous. I should do well." The other two pigs heard his stomach growl and said, "let's wait and walk farther. There is still a lot of daylight left."

The second pig continues to think and the third baby pig had made up his mind to follow his vision. The first pig said, "I am grown." Then he flopped down under a shade tree on a bright sunny day. He started eating his lunch. The other two pigs kept walking.

The first pig remembers visiting the town. He saw people living comfortably in straw huts. After a good nap the first pig got up and gathers his straws. Soon he built a beautiful straw hut. He even put in the necessary plumbing in case of a fire. And he added a back door, remembering that night, he added double locks. He was content.

The second pig was walking with the third pig. His stomach growled. The second pig said, "I know a carpenter in this area. I will visit him and build me a house of wood." The third pig knew once his brothers was hungry talking to them was useless. But he tried. The third pig said, "have you thought about a community with the three of us, it's possible for us to have a house together?" "We can pray together and help each other build a great house for each other." "Build a community for Christ and have the best." "I want to establish a homestead to have a family one day", said the third pig.

The second pig was already flopping down under a shade tree. The second pig nodded off and he told his brother, "hold that though…. Hmmm. I'll visit you latter." He ate his lunch and thought I will set up soon then took his nap. The third pig kept walking.

When the second pig woke, he went and traded for lumber. In a few days, he had his house built. It was done with a man cave in mind. Typical ranch style house was built. He made sure there was place for the latest video games, grill, and he decided to go all the way. He started digging for a pool. He knew his brothers would visit eventually. He thought life can be sweet. Remembering that night, he put in a solid wood door going to the outside with double the locks. He also uses safety windows with specific features and locks. Fears and doubts of leaving home were removed, the pig felt he had done well.

The third pig kept walking. Night time came upon him while he was still on the road. He found a place to rest. He said his prayers and slept. Upon morning, he ate breakfast then continued walking. That afternoon he knew he was at the right spot. It felt good. His spirit was high. His stomach growled but he knew he had to start his chores in a timely manner. He passed a brick making building. He knew his home would be built with bricks. After outlining his area for the house, he ate. When finished, he went back to work. He had a house built of brick with the latest, just as nice as his brothers. He especially likes to cook as well as the other brothers. He paid extra attention to his kitchen. He decides to add a chimney for those cozy nights with his future family.

After the three pigs built a roof over their heads, they began gardening. They planted difference trees., especially fruits trees. Their parents taught them how to plant. They used their knowledge wisely. They were happy. The first pig began to think about a wife. Second pig thought about teaching. He was very fond of gardening and herbs. He would love to teach others. Everything was put on hold when the weather turned bad. The third pig decided to add to his home so it will blend in with nature. He built shrubs and trees around his home. The landscape looks more like a park than a residential area. You would not know a home was there. The three pigs visited each other and life went on.

The big bad wolf was feeling his age. He knew he was not getting any younger. He had forgotten about the pigs village until he heard about the new neighbors and they were pigs. They were out in the country by their lonesome. This brought back memories. The wolf threw on his suit; it was loose but it fit. He thought just right for him, he was about to put some weight on. On the way, the wolf ran across a pig coming home. He forgot his rule about eating near home. So, anxious about his adventure that he pounced on the pig who tried to speak a good day to him as he did in town. The pig realizes too late and tried to run. But the wolf was upon him and devours him. He sheepishly looks around and realizes he was not seen. The wolf continued his way.

The wolf went to the first pig house. The pig saw the wolf coming from a distance. At first, he was not alarmed. He looks harmless. He looks like a dog. But he remembers the night of the wolf attack. He also remembers many was lost in their community due to being passive even after they realize they were dealing with a wolf. This pig knew they do not associate with wolves, and that they have a way of getting in your life and destroying it. He was not going to have any of that. He knew he had to believe and keep the hope that all will end well. Fear came over him, but it did not freeze him to his spot. It did the opposite. He dropped his hoe and ran back to his straw house, like his life depended on it.

The wolf saw him running. The wolf knew he could catch the plump pig, but he was not very hungry now. He wanted to savor the moment. When he got to the straw house, he will introduce himself. He asked, "can I come in?" The pig said, "NO." The wolf offered money, deals to die for, offered deals too good to be true, offered cheap land to sell from Florida, and then ask, "could I use your phone there no reception out here." The wolf did not have a phone. The wolf made his voice hoarse and asked, "may I have a glass of water". The pig turns around to get the water out of the kindness of his heart and quickly shook himself. The pig said, "no" as nicely as he could he hope the wolf would go away. The wolf wondered what was happening to good Samaritan these days.

The first pig knew the wolf was getting angry, but he was not ready to die. Out of desperation he started to pray. He asks the Lord for forgiveness for his lack of a prayer life. He felt strength and courage that he did not have before. He knew his prayers were being answer. That when he heard the wolf speak, "little pig, little pig let me come in."

"No No No not by the hair on my chinny chin chin" said the pig. The wolf said, "then I will huff, and I will puff, and I will blow your house in." The wolf put his all into the huff and the puff and blew out the air.

The wolf had not done this in a long time so he had a little doubt about his ability. He remembered well the night he was put to shame. He was humiliated by the elder speaking words of truth over him. He still believed the words had life in them. He believed the words took control of the situation and took it out of his hands.

To the wolf amazement he saw the house tilt and fall in. The wolf's confidence came back. Anger came over him. He felt big and bad again. So, he was determined to get to the pig before in the frenzy, thinking it might get away.

He dove into the straws. The first pig peeped out. At first the little pig did not seem to see the wolf. Then he must have noticed the wolf up front, because he headed to the back door. The wolf saw him and bit at him. He took off the tip of the pig's tail. The pig kept running. The pig made it to the back door. The pig slammed the door shut behind him; this brought the rest of the house down on the wolf. This jammed the wolf in the house. Then the pig ran because his life depended on it.

One can only imagine the disappointment of the wolf. It took a while to get untangled. He pulled himself together and headed in the direction of the pig. He wondered what to expect next. He felt sure about himself as he strode down the road that he would do better. "Wow another house!", said the wolf.

The first pig made a day journey in record time to the second pig's ` house. The second pig saw the first pig running toward him. He picks up his hoe and started running home. He didn't like the look of fear on his brother face. Better to be safe than sorry he thought to himself. No need to meet him since he was headed this way. "Never hurt to be cautious," thought the second pig near the door as he picked up his step to get to the door. The first pig caught up and neck to neck they ran to the door. The first pig would have past the second pig if he was not tired. Then he thought about the wolf. He looked behind and saw an outline in the distance and knew it was the wolf. He got his second wind. The first pig began to past the second pig. The second pig realized this and ran even faster. Inside the door, they ran and they got stuck in the doorway. It was a quick remedy the second pig elbowed the first pig and ran inside after his brother came in behind. The second pig began a lockdown of the house with the first pig's help. The first pig began to fill in the second pig what had happen. The second pig was furious that the first pig would lead the wolf to his house.

First pig thought to himself; "he would have done the same thing;" he did not want the second pig to throw him out. He kept that part silent. The first pig looked out his brother's window. He said, "I see him, I see the wolf coming down your road." Shutters and doors locked with latches thrown across the boards. The second pig thought I never thought to use the board across the door.

They became silent, they looked at each other trying to remember what to do next. They felt they were leaving something out. Something important. Then they felt confident they had the problem under control. They hoped the wolf would become discouraged and quickly leave.

The wolf continued to lop along to the second pig's house. Time had not been kind to him. Age had slowed him down. He was tired. He perked up when he saw the house. Life is finally being kind to me he thought to himself. The house is made of wood.

LINDA BRIDGES

He straightened out his suit. Walked up to the door and knocked. No need to get unnecessary winded, he remembered that straightforward approach work sometime because curiosity often kill the cat. The wolf was used to pigs falling for his lies. He felt he could reason with them. He asked, "Can I come in and use the phone and to drink a glass of chilly water to quench my dying thirst". The second pig squeaked, "no". The wolf asked, "why not?" "We could talk about it from pig to wolf" said the wolf. The second pig said, "no." The wolf could smell the fear coming out of the house. The wolf could smell two pigs in the house. He decides a different attack would work. He knew by now they were desperate. The wolf asks, "could one come out and discuss the proposition." He would settle with the other later, hoping one would sacrifice the other. Both pigs said, "no".

The second pig felt it would help discourage the wolf if he was truthful. He told the wolf how their parents raised them. He told the wolf about that dreadful night of the wolf attack and how prayers save them.

The wolf immediately remembered that night and grew furious. He felt the pigs had caused his misfortune throughout his life after that incident. Even though he knew inside truthfully that he destroyed the trust of those that dependent on him. He knew he enjoyed killing, stealing, and destroying. He knew there would be a reckon one day. He would reap what he had sowed. The wolf with the reprobate mind felt this would not be that day. The reprobate mind should also explain the dialogue he had with the pigs.

The wolf was tired of disappointments; he saw where this was going. He told the pigs firmly, "I am coming in!"

The pigs realize at the same time what they have missed. The first pig started to pray for the remission of his sins. He remembers what happened at his house. He wanted his house or life in order this time around. He wanted to do better.

The second pig heard him and realizes he's been slacking on his prayer life, too. He started to pray and tried to catch up with his brother's praying for his own sake. He asked for forgiveness. He promised he would do better and screamed SAVE ME LORD! The brothers continued to pray they did not see a way out.

The wolf hearing the commotion in the house, did not understand what they were saying. The brothers had begun to pray earnestly and in tongues. The wolf decided they were planning an escape and he began to speed up his plan. Little did the wolf know that his action was having the opposite effect. Instead of fearing, the pigs were regaining faith, hope, and most importantly love. A special touch from their Lord gave them grace and mercy and took load of weight off. (They would need it for the path ahead.)

The wolf said boldly, "little pig, little pig, let me come in." "No No No not by the hair on our chinny chin chin." Then I'll huff, and I'll puff, and I'll blow your house in," said the wolf. He was true to his word. The house tilted and fell in.

The pigs were terrified but not lock in their fear. The beams fell in around them they were barely missed. The second pig said, "follow me brother." He took him to a window. While the wolf was searching through the wood the pigs was going out the window. The second pig did not know that the wolf had sniffed them out. Close on their trail. The second pig let the first pig out first and closely followed. As he put his legs out the window first and the body followed he look up, face to face with the wolf. The wolf grinned and bit at the pig. The second pig without care threw himself out the window. Not fast enough for the wolf grabbed the pig's ear tip. That was all he grabbed. The pig slammed the window down and the rest of the house came down on the wolf. Buying them much needed time. They took off running neck to neck; they agreed "surely, we have found mercy." It was time to get to their third brother's house. As they neared the third pig's house, running with the wind and panting they were thankful they're still breathing. They were thankful for life. They ran on. They did not complain; they did not stop for water; they did not get hungry; and they continued to give thanks to the Lord.

Took a moment for the wolf to untangle himself and realized no pig was left. He thought this is unseemly when did pigs get smart and move so fast. How the time change. The wolf remembered they ran with a purpose down the road. "Away I go" he thought.

The first and second pigs saw their brother in the field as they got closer. They ran to him shouting. The fear of his brothers did not overwhelm him. He stopped working in his field. He thought I will call it a day. He tried to make out what his brothers were saying. They approached him screaming and hollering telling him about what had happen. He understood nothing they said. He followed them to his house. They ran past him. They tried to get in but the doors were locked. They had to wait on him. Noticing the calmest in their brother they begin to calm down. They realize they were still alive; they made it to their brother house and his house was made of brick.

The third pig made it to the door and let them in. As they finally calmed down they told their brother about the wolf. They told him it was the Big Bad Wolf from that night. The third pig said, "let's prepare." He said a prayer of protection. He particularly likes Psalm 91 where it said, "surely he will deliver us from the snare of the fowler and the noisome pestilence."

The third pig did not forget his prayer life. He had prayers stacked up for times like this. He wanted to continue to keep standing for what he believed in and not fall for anything. The third pig prayed as well as watch. He was ready. He believed the word be ye ready mean be ready. He made sure the doors were secure. He started cooking early and decided to grill in the chimney. He lit the fireplace which gave the house a calming atmosphere. Soon the food was ready to eat. They said, "God is good God is great, we do thank him for our food by His hands we are feed thank you Lord for our daily bread in Jesus name." "Amen". They gave thanks to the Lord for divine protection also. They did not find praying boring this time.

They started eating and remembered their parents talking. Many families disappeared now we know why. They remembered the bones found at the wolf house. They were afraid, but not frozen in their fear. The third pig reminded them and said, "we are not given the spirit of fear, but of love, power, and a sound mind. We must hold fast to our integrity." The third pig said, "we must not become divided but be of same mind and honest to each other." "Most importantly do not leave this house until the battle is over," said the third pig.

The third pig knew what his house stood on, not just a man-made foundation, but on the Rock. The other houses were good houses but they were built on sand.

There was a knock on the door. The pigs stopped eating. The wolf was hungry and tired. The wolf was feeling lucky. He straightened his suit. He knew this should work. The suit was dusty but it would get his point across. The wolf cuts through the chase. He got straight to the point. "Let's make a deal, I am a wolf with many opportunities; could I interest you in a deal?" The third pig said firmly, "no!" The wolf said, "since you would not let me in could you step out?" The third pig said strongly, "NO!"

The wolf pulled himself up. He felt good about himself because he had eaten one pig, blew down two houses. He was thinking time to wrap this up.

The third pig said, "let us pray a prayer of victory." Not a prayer of repentance, he always does that. They knew about the Lord's control over the winds. Then they spoke to the wind, "Be calm in Jesus name." Because they knew this day their enemy would be delivered to them.

The wolf said, "are you so sure." "Little pig, little pig, will you let me come in,' sweetly said the wolf. "No No No not by the hairs of our chinny chin chin," said the pigs. "Then I'll huff, and I'll puff, and I'll blow your house down," said the wolf. And the wolf blew. Nothing happen. The wolf blew his strongest puff yet. When the dust cleared, the house was standing. The third pig had to calm his brothers because they were ready to flee out of the house. They almost ran out of their safety ark the brick home. When the pigs saw the power of prayer at work; hope, faith, and charity was restored. The pigs remembered their upbringing and vows not to stray again.

The wolf was not through with them. The wolf tried three times to blow the house down. The wolf was stunned and exhausted. The house was still standing. He knew he had blown bigger houses down. Why was this one different from the other? Then he heard it, clearly, not only prayer, but those words. He never knew words could carry power. The words where He arose and rebuked the winds and the sea, and there was a great calm. The wolf now knew what had defeated him. He felt he had to move quickly. Still thinking with his stomach and not his heart; the wolf did not repent. He saw an opening. The wolf started for the chimney feeling defeat settling in his stomach, but he would not accept that. He's been around the house but everything was seal shut. The house was well made, seal, and kept clean. The wolf could not break in. The wolf climbed the house to the chimney. He thought, "I should try this more often this is simple." He was so anxious he did not feel the heat of the chimney, nor smell the fresh smoke. He thought, "after I devour the pigs I will rest in this house." He threw his body into the pipe of the brick chimney. First it was easy going, but soon got tight. He started to wiggle down the chimney. He felt like he would barely make it.

The pigs had blank the fire in the chimney, but heard the noise coming from the chimney. They knew what was happening. The wolf was close. The third pig with the help of his brothers rebuilt the fire in the fireplace. One stirs the coals, another added more wood, while the other blew air to quicken the flame.

The wolf felt heat and realized what was happening. He tried very hard to stop himself from going down. He saw life before his eyes and it was not good, yet he could not stop. He realized he had started something he could not halt. As his life flashed before his eyes, it was not fruitful. He also realized people had shown his kindness, love, and feed him when he was hungry; and in returned he betrayed them over and over. He mourned, "Oh woe is me!".

The wolf was so intent on getting down the chimney he did not bother with a way to get back up. He realized he had been foolish. The wolf did not stand a chance. When he knew, he had made his bed and was about to die in it, he started howling, and pleading, but it was soon over.

The pigs kept their word and built a community pleasing to the Lord. They built a house of worship and the goodness of the Lord flourish throughout the land.

THE END

Jack And The Beanstalk

There was once a lovely couple. They had a son named Jack. Jack is a typically young boy. You could say he could be your son in his teenage years. These were tough times, they didn't have much. But they knew how to stretch what they had and gave thanks to the Lord. The cupboard always had something in them. They managed to have their needs met. But time continue to get hard. The Father had to go farther to get what they needed. He knew people were desperate, they all had needs.

Food was scarce. Jack's Father went to fetch a cow. He barely got the cow home. He had to travel mostly at night. He could not bring the few packages home. He knew he was being followed and had to move fast. He feared to take Jack, he was all they had. "Soon Jack must learn the trade, he thought. He was going to get around to it. Unfortunately, that night Jack's Father went to retrieve the packages of food that was hid. That same night Jack's Father was killed.

So Jack grew up without his Father. However, he was not a bad child, just laid back and too smart for his own good. He was known to overthink a problem. He always thought he could do better than what his mother told him. He stressed out the cow, lost a pig, left the chicken coop door open through the night. His mother and father prayed on. While his Father was still living he allowed Jack to be baptized, when the minister passed through their valley they had Jack baptize in the name of Jesus.

He loved lying under the oaks. One-day Jack was daydreaming in the shade about his father when he sadly remembered he was no longer alive. Jack knew he had to grow up. He had to become the breadwinner, to mature. Then he thought, "not yet."

Jack's mother called, "Jack, Jack come to the house." She yells, "Oh Jack." She had an important errand for him to run. Time had been hard on his mom. She was unable to do long walks and heavy chores. She was dependent on Jack, for him to help make end meet. She was a praying woman she kept the faith. It was slow but she saw the maturity growing in Jack. Not leaving it completely to Jack, she sent up prayer requesting for her son to be the man the Lord wanted him to be. She believed in Jack or she would take the cow and sell it herself. She said, "Jack go to bed early; rest well." "You will have to leave early in the morning." She told him, "I need you to sell the cow and buy what on this list." She gave him a list of things to buy. She said, "stay focus."

Jack knew the importance of selling the cow. He was going to bed hungry. Jack was a daydreamer. Daydreaming was not filling his stomach. Jack could dream at night just as well as day. Jack dreamed of eating his favorite dishes. For a moment, all was well. As dreams come and go. Jack awakens to his growling stomach. His mom was waiting for him with a crust of bread. "Morning Ma", Jack said. Mother said, "Morning Jack, here breakfast, stay on the road." "Jack, I'm depending on you," mother said.

Jack's mom watched him walk off. She said a silent prayer of protection, health, strength, knowledge, and wisdom for Jack. She knew that he knew his way there because the road went straight to the town. The walk was long. She thought, "the price for the cow would feed us well for a while." Mom said to herself, "if the clouds would rain, there would be grass for the cow and my garden would produce." "Grace and mercy Lord." She waved at Jack and watched him pull the cow down the road. She walked back in the house saying, "we will make it."

Jack waved goodbye to his mom. Jack was thinking on how to get the most for the cow. Jack daydreamed of getting chickens, beans, bread, and having coins left over. The challenging times was not over yet. As Jack was walking down the road he thought he heard whistling and he did. Jack was in his own little world (daydreaming).

The man noticed Jack coming down the road with a cow. The man also happened to need a cow. He had many mouths to feed. He was an honorable man but had fallen on demanding times. Once he was well known for his green thumb. People would travel for miles to learn how to make their gardens grow to the extreme. His advice was priceless. As the man approached Jack, he whistled to get the boy's attention. He had to whistle louder.

The man approached Jack and was noticed. The man stated, "what a fine cow; young man what are you going to do with that cow." Jack was excited. He said, "I was going to trade it in at the market."

The man thought, "I don't know about the market but I need that cow. The man cunningly said, "that's all? Surely you can do better than that." "I was going to the market to trade these beans in. Each bean can grow large beans on the bush with four times the beans by four." He watches Jack's expression. He then said, "plant these beans and you will never go hungry." Jack's stomach was growling. He thought, "I might swap them out for the cow. I guess I can drop the price."

As the man talked numbers Jack's eyes lit up. He thought, "mom and him can eat forever off those beans." Jack considers himself to be as smart as the next fellow. Jack put his two-cent in. Jack said, "I am going to the market to make a deal and you are going to the market to make a deal. Let's make a deal here." He shares his bread with the stranger. Then Jack thought about it and swaps the cow for the beans. Jack thought, "wow what a great deal!"

The man liked the way Jack thinks. Jack and the man traded. Jack took the beans while the man took the cow.

The man wiped the nervous sweat from his forehead and said, "Whew, that was close, I really needed that cow." He knew that if the boy kept faith and be courageous and stayed kind he will not be disappointed.

They went their separate ways. Jack was glad he did not have to travel to town. He rushed home to give his mom the fantastic news.

Jack's mom almost fainted. She was furiously. Then she saw red. Jack's mother exercised her parental shouting rights. She screamed at Jack trying once again to explain their difficult life. She said, "it was not always like this, but surely you know we are about to starve." After a hyper moment, she calmed down. She realized this was her only son. As they came in the world with nothing it looked like they would certain leave with nothing. It was in God's hand.

"The cow was all we had left," she said, "Jack the cow was solid, it was something you could put your hands on, it was there. We could have eaten it if necessary." The mom knew trading it for what they needed was the best option. She decided to stop crying over spilled milk. "The beans," she said, "the four beans might or might not grow." She threw the beans out the window.

He was upset with himself. Disappointment is a bitter pill Jack thought. That evening Jack grew up. Jack knew he had to do something to help his mom. He saw her in a different light. He saw the tiredness, the worrying, and the love despite all he has done and did not do.

When Jack went to sleep that night, he prayed for a miracle. He wanted to help his mom. He now wanted to become a man that she can be proud of. As Jack slept he thought he felt the house shake. He ignored it on. Jack woke up early. As he went outside to look at the start of a day, thinking of a way to lift the burden offs his mom. Jack saw a tree. That was not there last night. Then he remembered the beans.

Curiosity got the best of him, he knew he had to climb this tree. He saw giant beans hanging off the tree. The tree seemed to go up forever. It looked like it went through the clouds. "Wow!" Jack said. Jack cut a few of the beans off the tree for his mom. Jack grabbed a water bag. He was ready to climb. He started up the tree. As Jack climbed he noticed four vines twisted together to make the tree sturdy. On he climbed farther and was beginning to tire he climbed through clouds. Yet the tree went on. Jack looked up and Jack looked down, then Jack look around. To Jack surprise he saw land. Jack's curious nature got the best of him.

He got off the tree and followed a path he found. To Jack's amazement he saw a massive house. It was made from wood and stone. "Wow", Jack thought, "this is an enormous house, gigantic people must stay here!" Jack could barely believe his eyes, he saw a garden, pond, and well it looks like a farm. Jack couldn't wait to get inside. Jack squeezes under the door. To his amazement again, he thought, "this house might be a castle." It was royally decorated and Jack saw food on a large table. He saw a large chair. Then he saw it. Coins! Gold coins in all sizes. Jack ate, drank water, and grabs some coins. In the coins was a golden egg. Jack grabs it too. Jack squeezed under the door and left the big house. As Jack was leaving he thought, "he felt the ground shaking, then he remembered he was in the sky, walking on a cloud. He murmurs, "it must be the wind."

He took his time and climbed down the tree. He approached his mom with good news. Once his mom understood what Jack was saying, she remembered to breathe. Mom had to relook at the tree. She realized Jack said he climbed the tree and found gold. Mom was excited. Mom was also hungry. All she could think about was how they were going to eat a proper meal and getting repairs on the house, building up the farm, and so much more. She thought a blessing fell from heaven.

She had Jack to get the neighbor from down the road that did chores for them when they could afford it. He had his own family to care for and was on tough times. She could pay him to run her errand. Jack was relieved to see the relief on his mother face. She remembered she must ask Jack where he got the gold.

A few days and Jack was content. A few days' latter curiosity got the best of Jack. He grabbed his bags and climbed up the tree. As Jack sneaked up the tree he remembered what his mom told him. She told him about the legends of the giants that stole from their land below and how they somehow always escaped up in the clouds. She told Jack, "not to go back."

As Jack reached the big house no one seemed to be at home. But inside Jack met a woman. She was much taller than him and his mom. Before Jack could speak she knew he was there. She could smell Jack. She was pleased to see him. The tall woman asked, "who's here that I smell?" Jack stepped up and introduced himself. Remembering his manner. Jack said, "hello, I did not know all this was here." Jack asked, "could I fish in the pond." The woman immediately answers, "No!" She said, "my husband is not a kind man and is very impatient." She laughed and said, "that putting it mildly." The woman was desperate for company. She made small talk and fed him well. The woman warned Jack about the Giants that live here. They were all dangerous. She told Jack, "do not stay long." She told him, "my husband is a mean man; he cannot find you here." As she was talking to Jack he saw a goose and to his amazement the goose laid a golden egg. As the woman turned around Jack fed the goose bread crumbs and snatches it. He placed the goose in his bag. He heard the door opening. And felt footstep. Jack hid.

The Giant had returned home from seeding his ground in the sky. His garden could produce an abundant from the extra water he drew in.

Unlike the woman, the Giant was careful about what he ate. The Giant miss his main ingredient for his bread. Upon entering the castle, he senses a person nearby so he spoke this rhyme.

"Fee-Fi-Fo-Fum!
I smell the blood of a holy one
Be he alive, or be he dead
I'll grind his bones to make my bread."

The woman told her husband, "stop thinking with your stomach. Come eat." When the Giant got full he fell asleep. Jack grabbed the goose and escaped down the beanstalk.

When the Giant awakened, He already knew he was missing several gold coins. He knew because he counted them often. He was also familiar with the weight. He noticed he did not hear the goose cackling. The Giant screamed, "IT IS GONE!" The Giant was furious. He fussed at the woman who claimed to not know anything. She lied and said, "I did not see anyone." The woman thought, "foolish boy, he has a death wish." She hoped he would not come back.

The woman knew the Giant came by those items many years ago, when he could go back and forth in the land of the small men. The Giants stole and took much. The Giants storm the human land. They ate up the livestock and humans too. When they drink water, they would empty rivers and lakes. Then they started uprooting the trees and stealing humans to take with them. The land was still recovering from the brutal attack. It is not known what drove the Giants back into the clouds and made them stay there. Jack had an idea. When they destroy the land, they destroy the nourishments for the giant trees that exist at that time. The trees must have been their transportation. That was when Giants walked among the men. The woman missed the company. She missed any company. There were not many giants. Matter of fact her Giant was more prosperous than the other few. She always thought they quickly come and quickly go.

Jack got the confused goose home. He kept the goose close for the next few days. He noticed the goose laid a golden egg a day. Jack was talking to the trees and said, "How am I going to break the news to mom." Then she would know he'd go back up the tree. He added the few golden coins to the cookie jar. His mom realized the cookie jar had more coins. She said sternly, "do not go back Jack and I mean just that!"

One day the goose got loose. It was in the yard when his mother spotted it. Jack did not know the goose was loose. Mom immediately remembered her lean days. She believed, "waste not want not, it had to be more blessings sent from heaven." Jack's mom caught the goose. She prepared a feast with the goose being the main course. Usually she used turkey but goose would do as well. Plus, it was Jack's favorite dish. She learned it from Mama Regina. Jack was depressed only for a moment. Then he realized there was a lot of good from this meal. He did not have to tell his mom he went back up the beanstalk. Wow! What a great meal it was.

Several days went by; Jack thought more about the castle. He remembered the gold but there was a golden harp that played by itself. That would be a wonderful gift for mom, Jack thought. At least that was his excuse for going back up the stalks.

The Giant had a suspicious nature and found the tree; he wondered where it came from. He also noticed the vines came through the clouds. He had not forgotten his time visiting the small men. He found them to be capable of self-preservation. The Giant kept an eye on the tree. He knew there was a sneaky intruder; he did not misplace his possession. Beside the goose was too lazy to leave. It's been a long time but he began to remember men. He knew what the intruder was. He became watchful.

Jack climbed the beanstalk a third time. Jack kept repeating to himself, "this will be my last time." Jack knew he was taking a big chance. He prayed, "one more time Lord." Jack grabbed extra bags and placed the axe by the beanstalk. He did not trust his willpower and what he might run into. So, he was going to cut the stalks down. As he began to climb the stalks he thought, "what will I grab and how will I say goodbye to the woman."

Jack peeped over the clouds. He did not see any one. Little did Jack know the Giant had found the beanstalks. Daily the Giant sniffed for Jack's return, and watched the beanstalk. As Jack approached the big house. The Giant smelled him from the field. He started to the house.

The woman did fuss at Jack for returning. She told him, "you are foolish to come back; the Giant knows you were here." Jack said, "I thank you for your kindness and I will not be returning."

This got Jack's attention. This also frightened Jack instead of dilly dallying he sped things up. Jack felt like he had overstayed his welcome. He realized what the woman was saying was true. He also realized greed got the best of him. He had been foolish to come back, but he did not want to leave empty handed. As soon as the woman turned toward the stove, he grabbed the harp and some coins and ran for the door.

When the woman turned around, fussing, "you are a foolish boy playing with death." The woman knew without a doubt the Giant would eat him. Jack took off for the door. The woman thought she would not mind cooking a chicken or she meant a boy pot pie. They had not had one in a while.

The Giant came through the door. The door did bam open. Jack jumped behind the broom. The Giant came in smiling. The woman was at the stove. The Giant started singing,

"Fe-Fi-Fo-Fum!

I smell the blood of a holy one

Be he alive or be he dead

I'll grind his bones to make my bread."

He lost the scent. He started sniffing to find Jack. The woman said not a word. The Giant was anxious and quickly passed by Jack. The dusty broom helped for a moment to hide his scent. The Giant went past Jack. Jack came out and scooped under the door and started to run. He ran like his life depended on it. As he got closer to the beanstalk, thinking he might escape this without too much sweat, the harp began to play. The Giant's ears heard the harp. The Giant shouted, "I hear my harp outside the house." "My harp is not in the house." The man had stolen his harp.

Jack gulped and knew this would be the run of his life. He knew trouble was upon him. Jack doubled his speed. Even he did not know he had it in him, his life flashed before his eyes at this moment. He did not like what he saw. He told something, "I will do better." He admits to himself he knew who something was; it was God.

He knew he needed to run faster. He began to drop bags and empty his pockets. Jack knew he had to lighten his load. Jack knew he was at fault. This was not a time to lie to himself. Jack said an out of breath prayer, "I repent for my sins, especially the sin of greed, laziness, selfishness, and so many others, oh Lord, so many. Please forgive me, I will do better." Jack dropped sinful weights. Jack ran even faster. Somehow, he didn't have time to wonder how his hope was restored. Jack leaped on the beanstalk scooping and dropping down as fast as he could. He noticed a thump on the beanstalk. He did not have to guess; he knew that the Giant was following.

Jack saw the ground getting closer. He screamed, "Ma Ma", "grab the axe and start chopping." Hearing the terror in her son's voice she did just that. As Jack neared his mom he jumped a little way down the beanstalk. He grabbed the axe from his mom and started chopping for his life depended on it and it did. The Giant was still a way up the beanstalk. When he almost had it chopped, the beanstalk began to tilt over from the weight of the Giant. The beanstalk fell over. The Giant was killed from the fall of the stalk.

It started to sprinkle and later it rained. This shocked Jack and his mom.

Jack never let his greed get the best of him again. Jack became the son his mom longed for. Jack regained his prayer life and always gave thanks to the Lord. He knew divine intervention save him that day. He knew the Lord restored his hope and true dreams. He could keep putting one foot in front of the other. Missing his dad did not hurt as much. Jack stopped looking down on his life. Jack had a happy life in the Lord.

THE END

understand now how those close to you can be can be more dangerous than strangers and how we are our own worst enemy. I have a large family. Some is sticking to the living word. And some have decided that this is not the time the bible warns us about in Revelation. We have separated. I still pray for them.

I could clearly see my downfall if I stay with my family. My love for my family fill with good intentions.

Notice my way, my good intentions. Knowing I cannot save anyone. Thank God for dealing with me early in my spiritual growth. I learn to obey first and trust him in all things. Yes, I am still growing. I have family issues. Some walk side by side with death and know what God has saved them from. They learned to trust God blindly; they have faith. The Lord saved them in dangerous mess; you can surely see trial and tribulations have given us faith.

I obey and keep praying because there are those that refuse to acknowledge the Lord as their Savior no matter what he has done for them. They call out to me to help just a little until they get on their feet. Simple things that would not have taken much, but I obeyed God. I stood still and prayed and encourage them with the living word. I see God moving in their lives.

The word tells us those in sin and have repented will out run the ones in the church buildings coming to God. Saving themselves from this untoward generation. We live with a generation of vipers and tares, they have always been here. The enemy sowed many tares with the bloodline of Cain. When the enemy convinced Cain to eliminate his brother it gave Cain's bloodline a head starts and the enemy tried many times to dilute King David's bloodline to not avail. As we are being children of faith, we know there is nothing too hard for God. John the Baptist and Jesus called them out. I know the time that I am living in.

I had to deny them. I do not keep in touch with some of them. I remembered the reasons. They brought strangers into my home to explain the changes coming. Emphasizing how harmless it is. It was then I realized many have already sold out from Christ. They talk like this is a done deal. They were courteous, considerate, and foolishly I tried to be the perfect hostess. They did not know when to leave. They kept coming back. Encouraging me to conform to this world is how I saw it. My mind was already transformed by the living word. (Roman 12:1). I told them what they could do with the ideas for the future. I told them they control the chips in cards, our pets, and electronics that should be enough. They assure me the rewards would be reasonable and there would be many perps. I escorted them out. Oh, the deceit, they acted like they are helping me.

I prayed when they left. I ask Father God in Jesus name to send confusion to the enemy's camp do not let them find my house. I asked, "Lord give me the strength to stand what to come and I ask Father God to send Godly people only to my residence." That restore my peace of mind.

I have been asked to speak at the next meeting. We try to allow everyone to have a turn to tell how they are holding to their faith. I think we all agree to the time we are in. I will be led by the Spirit. I will obey. I will speak. This is what I believe.

First, I asked them is the mark of the beast a fact or fiction? One should know the mark of the beast is very real, it is important that we do not receive this mark. They will prefer the right hands or head to put it in. This is where they will require it to be as stated in the bible. Why because we know what is written, will be done. Make you wonder why on the right hand and head? Man consider the right hand and forehead because we move it a lot and it will keep the lithium battery in the chip charged up. Any part of the body should do. You must remember Satan takes orders from God. It is written and in the word of God and it will be done. This should let's know without doubt who's in charge.

The mark will be the mark of the antichrist and will allow people to buy and sell to the public, good housing, see the doctors, free child care, and all about identification, location, and the money, etc. It will seem to make their life extremely easy and comfortable; some will have superhuman strength, healing, and feeling, but it will past and they will develop beast like behavior. The chip will carry an evil genetic code to change your DNA at a genetic level; you will no longer be human. You will lose your soul. Sound science fiction; now you see were the movies come from . They have desensitized us. The enemy has conditioned many minds to think this is a small matter, because we are programed to follow this world. They say the mark or chips are safe. They are in our pets, cards, cell phones, foods, and many other items. They told us it will not hurt. The area can be numb. Many will think nothing of it; they may liken it to get a tattoo or an extra piercing. But it is the mark of the beast which give us the image of the beast only a chip? No! The taking of the chip signifies you denouncing Jesus and will lead to biological changes. Your worst horrible movie coming to life. You have sold out because you verbally and in your actions, canceled Jesus out of your life or you are in sin. You have bowed to the image of the beast. To thinks anything of you are left is a lie, you have vacated your premises. You have left your house (body). It is occupied. It is done; you are damned.

Don't think the mark of the beast have just begun; it has been happening for years. Some of us are just waking up spiritually to reality as the bible want us to see. The veil removed off our eyes. The mark or tattoo is not the only danger in losing your soul. If you do not have Jesus you are already lost. If you are acting outside the characteristics of Jesus you are lost. It the fruits of the Holy Spirit that will give us the characteristics of Jesus. Where is your faith? Where is your humility? Where is your love? Where is your forgiveness? This should be alive in you now to be ready.

It is frightening to realize that many already have the attitude (carnal mind) of the world thus they carry or bow to the image of the beast. Through ignorance they have received the mark of the beast. They are ready for the picking by the enemies. No resistance, they will be lead like sheep to the slaughter.

Why such a lack of resistance? We are not only attacked spiritually but physically. Our bodies are being deprived of it essential nutrients or building blocks (trace elements). Our body is being broken down at a molecular DNA level we do not see. The government tell us all is well and many continue to believe them. Some try to change their diet, but it's too late. The spiritual damage is done as well as physical; you must trust Jesus to keep you whole and carry you through. The drive, motivation, strength, challenges to ask question and fight if necessary is lacking. It's all in the enemy's plans. We will take a law or order without questions thus we will be like sheep lead to the slaughter if we do not repent and trust Jesus.

They have poisoned the air, water, animals, plants, and us. They sprayed chem trials (trials of chemicals) in the air, they have put dead fetuses in our vaccination and other unwanted things we would not consume knowingly. There are Nano bytes naturally found in nature in small amount, they have taken the nanobytes and tamper with them now they are in our body and programed to break it down.

There is nothing created that our Father did not create. All that Father created was good including us; unfortunately, we did not leave it that way. So, the enemy must use what on hand or what we have in our ignorance, knowingly have given to him. The only way to not look like the world is to have God's spirit.

The Lord says his children shall worship Him in Spirit and in Truth (John 4:23). They love and have truly forgiven.

The love of the world has wax cold (Matthew 24:12). The world is rebellious, lies, extort, hate, backstab, envy, bully, sew discord, and so many others, but it does loves its own (John 15:19).

❋ ❋ ❋

The Spirit revealed to me that the enemy was taking people out before their time. They were dying before their times. You think it is not possible. I heard several with testimonies that they died and went to hell. When they realized where they were they called out to Jesus and he delivered them out. Because they were His; they had faith. Those that do not belong to Jesus or had no faith stayed, they belonged to Satan.

You might ignorantly agree to a piercing, mark or tattoo but have not delicate your life to Christ then you enslave yourself to Satan. (Hopefully it not the mark of the beast then you are damn). But to go into the end of the ends days without Jesus is automatically damnation. The mark of the beast will keep you from changing your mind until it too late especially with the spirit of distraction on a rampage. If the elect barely makes it in what about those left behind? Do not be left behind! Plus, they have not mentioned what's in the chips, or the injections that will be given. I ask, "Truly do you want to lose your soul and lose the image of the Father in you and take on the image and form of the beast?"

We are mentally and physically programed to fail. It started when Adam and Eve committed sin. The Serpent stole their blessing. He took this world from man. He began to design it for our failure. Every time a sin is committed it opens a doorway for the enemies to come into our realm and now sin is on a rampage. Thus, what we see now is an illusion around us and we cannot trust anything we see. We are addicted to electronics, foods, microwave gratifications, and other things we are not even aware of. Many know this and continue this path of destruction. The flesh is weak but the spirit is willing. The enemy control our flesh; they can make us happy, sad, angry, and destructive. Don't believe it; go without gadgets such as cell phone for less than a day; or go without juke food for a day. You could pass out or wake up in a mental institution.

What can we do? Trust only Jesus. Lean not toward our own understanding but in all things, acknowledge the Lord and He will direct our path (Proverb 3:5). This earth is just a step over, a preparation place soon we will be angels. We must hold out. We need to study to show ourselves approved so we will not be ashamed. We can do all things through Christ Jesus who strengthen us.

I remembered the Jews were tattooed with barcodes, slaves with their masters' brand like an animal. Hebrews had slaves and in the seventh year had to release them. If they chose to stay they had a ring place through their nose showing ownership. Many are carrying piercings and rings and have not repented and delicated their life to Christ then you belong to Satan. (Exodus 21:5,6). There is a meaning to all our actions. If you are still breathing you have free will, make the right chose.

Many Jews wear their barcode today to remember and helped other to remember the Holocaust; hopefully to keep many from being desensitize from the truth. Their actions mean something. And slavery is very active in the world today. Many chose not to follow the word of God and say they believe in him. We must stand for truth (something real) or we will fall for anything.

Many people are coming up missing. Even now we believe there are concentration camp made from big building. That many people are being sent to them because they will not conform. They will not agree to take the mark of the beast. If they say help is over here even if it is a reputable rescue camp, stay put or be ready to run because it could lead to encampment.

The truth will set us free. I acknowledge that there are many things I have yet to learn but Yahshua is God, there is a heaven and a hell, called nothing God made common for he made all. I came to realization that the Hebrews calendar starts a new month at every full moon; our days of the weeks are screwed up by the enemy. Don't get caught up in the deception of whose, what, she said, he said; but talk to God and Truth. (Colossians2:7,8,15,16,18). This will keep you out of the confusion in the world. There is a lot of confusion. The enemy does not want us to know we are grafted into the Olive Tree by the blood of Christ. We must know the truth about God. We must trust in God. Do you really know the God you serve? If we do not trust God he cannot save us, so we must know his Truth(Son).

The mark can be a deception of the true word of God. He wants us to blaspheme. The enemy wants the word of God compromised. He wants us to attack God's creditably (to question or doubt God). Then we will lose trust. Remember his people perish from lack of knowledge. We must believe and keep the faith.

* * *

What is faith? Minister Ewing sum up faith as faith + work = the will of God. How did he come to this? Roman 10:17 states faith come by hearing, and hearing by the word of God. It is saying faith is the word of God. You must believe in God's word, the Son, and all he stands for to please God. I also strongly believe in my spiritual man and the spiritual realm, because we were raised around witchcraft and spirits. God was not short of his word He saved us. God is true to his word, able to do all things but fail.

How will we survive? I am learning a new meaning to faith. I have found areas where I was short. I thought I had the faith of a mustard seed and was doing well. Surprised by trials and tribulations that showed me up. I have blessed assurance that faith is rooted in me now. Thanks to the Lord!

I see the falling away in the churches occurring. Many do not have the faith of a mustard seed and are not aware. They are caught up in pride, stubbornness, hardheaded, and stiff necks, they fail to hear and see the warnings from God. There is always a warning before destruction. Plus, many churches tell their members to follow the church rules and they are saved; they leave church with no changes. They come looking for that security from the church and nothing from God. They feel safe in the world thinking they will have their cake and eat it too.

Without faith, you cannot please God or serve him. God will meet our needs have faith. The Just shall live by faith. David wrote these words wisely, "I have never seen the righteous forsaken or beg for bread." Yes, faith will feed us and keep our soul intact.

✻　✻　✻

Exactly what is this mark? Some say it is the essence of the mind or what you believe in, tattoo of 666, or a chip. One thing is for sure it is here and if you receive it you are damned.

Let's reflect on Mark 12:16, 17. When you spend money it represents the image of its owner. In this case Caesar's money carried Caesar's image, he requires you to pay him for it uses. That part of what you had belonged to Caesar. He charged taxes for the use of his money and the protection it gives. In case we do not know who money it is he stamped his image on it.

Our money is similar today. It has images on it but not on us. We pick it up and we put it down but we also have a choice. We spend as much or as little of this money as we want to. Do we spend a little or a lot; can we borrow a little or a lot; we should pay it back. One can become indebted to this system. It can get messy. Money takes on many difference appearances now. It can be balance out if greed stays out of the picture. Then we do not have to become enslave to debt. (By the way this is a sin).

When we take the mark of the beast or the image of the beast; we are the currency. You have been disobedient and you have sold your soul and given up your salvation. You no longer belong to yourself or to Jesus. You have sold your life, soul, and privacies to the enemy. They know more about you than you do. You are damned! Yes, the Father is omnipotence; knows all and his word is true. There are things between God and his saint that only God and his saint share. Our relationship with God through his Son is personal, private, and yet revealing. The anointing shows. It shows in our life.

We know the chance of receiving the mark is great. To be relieved of all debts. There will be a remnant that will be awakened and think debts or no debts; I do not want to go to hell. If it was possible the very elect would be deceived. They will not receive the mark. They will ask for forgiveness and repent to the Lord and be true. We can prepare ourselves from most of this now. There will be drastic changes even to the point of going homeless, get out of debts, but we can make the right choice. There will be bills, but there a difference between abusing funds and daily bills (utilities and such). Will we obey God?

In chapter 13 of Revelation the bible clearly states we should not receive this mark if you do you are damned. The pressure will be on the saints to stay steadfast some secretly and some not so secretly in the Lord. I guess we will be like Nicodemus seeking and believing in Jesus (John 3), but believing and living in him sincerely. Our faith will be put to the test, which is why we pray for the mind of Christ to be in us to enable us to stand. We will bear our cross and we will drink from the cup and be steadfast in obeying His word. His word is hiding in our hearts so we do not sin against Him. The battle starts in the mind. Do not lose faith for we can do all things through Jesus Christ who strengthen us!

The mark is the continuation of the separation of God's children from the devil's children and more. There is no turning back. The bible states the wheat will be separated from the tare or the sheep from the goats. There will be no lukewarm for Jesus. There will be no doubt who you worship. There will be no rock to hide under. Which one are we? You will know which one you are if you do not know now. You probably heard rumors about life end in the grave, or they been saying Jesus coming back and he have not come back yet, or this one - there is no hell. God 's word is being fulfill. He will be back. Everyone will know with absolute certainty the complete truth of the living word.

The enemy has been planting tares in God's wheat for a long time. He does it when we are sleep or awake. He can place things in our minds, life when we are busy and not giving God his due, in many many ways. It will take the blood of Christ to wash us clean. Please let Jesus finish his work. The Blood does not just wash us cleaned at a molecular level, but spiritually as well. Things from our childhood, ancestors, that we are not aware of is wash clean by the Blood. There will be no excuse. People you think are real for Christ; could be a tare. Trust Jesus. Persecutions will help us to decide whom we will serve. If we serve God we will get closer to God. If not, it will drive that person away.

＊ ＊ ＊

I am preparing myself to live a life with Christ in his Heaven. No more crying, sickness, worrying, hunger, etc. Not on the day of the rapture but now. I want to be ready. My purgatory is this earth, the preparation place. When I leave this earth, it will be death, sleep, or in the rapture. I give my spirit to Jesus.

Many are preparing for this place but I do not see the signs in their life. Many want to live forever? You will live eternally, but where? Heaven or hell? Good news! Hell, is not a place where we have to go it was not made for us, but for the fallen angels (demon) and Lucifer. We can make our choices. The trick is having knowledge. Knowing you are making choices if you speak or not speak. If you stand neutral, you are making a choice. You are still, undecided, standing, but your road (life) is still moving and taking you with it. You may not have made that choice. Your choice is being made for you by your flesh or Satan. Are you lukewarm (doubtful) or have you invited Jesus in?

No one in their Christ like mind wants to go to hell. Satan does not want to go there. Many are on their way to hell with all the intentions of going to heaven. Having good intention but not living an obedience life in the word will not get you in heaven. Good intentions will not get any of us to heaven only Christ.

Through history we see sign of the enemy attempting to imitate our Lord. The mark is no different. It is one of the most subtle, dangerous attempts yet. It will seal you to the antichrist. It will make him your Master and you will be lost.

The Lord placed a seal on us through the Holy Spirit. We have a reason to rejoice. (2 Corinth 1:22). We are sealed by the Holy Spirit with the promises of God fully intact

(Ephesians 1:13, 4:30). The Holy Spirit preserve us until the great day of the Lord, even when we cease to breath we do not die but sleep in the Spirit of the Lord, awaiting His call. Our redemption occurred when we accept the cross (Jesus), we believe.

Why is it important to be sealed? It means we are established, determined, unchangeable, and secured from being tamper with by the enemy. That is good news. We cannot be possessed by demons. We are private property to evil. The plagues will pass us by. We are practicing what we are preaching and preaching what we are practicing. You are a candle not hid under a basket. You are a holy light in a murky world that has not realize it is darkening. You are living a holy life. We suffer to reign with the Lord. We are surpassing our trials and tribulations gracefully with mercy in Jesus we pray. Our seal cannot be broken unless we (disobey) lose faith in the will of the Lord.

This does not mean we are weaponless. Our weapon is mighty to the pulling down of stronghold. It is the word of God. Gain the Lord's wisdom and knowledge so you will know how to use it by faith. Knowledge to use the wisdom He gives us is essential. It is our weapon.

Therefore, the enemy will come and we will have an opportunity to receive his red-carpet treatment. He will attempt to steal our hope, destroy our belief, or kill us. This is not a secret. It is the only truth the Father of lies will uphold. The Lord Jesus has spoken these words on him and it is true. It is occurring every day. Remember we are not weaponless. You will get first class lies and temptations to step out of the will of the Lord. The enemy cannot get to you; he wants you to come to him. (You are in the palm of God hand and the devil cannot pluck you out). If you disobey, please repent for the remission of your sins from the heart. He loves us so much he will forgive us. But if you receive the mark of the beast he still loves you, but he cannot save you.

The Lord knows who are His for they have departed from sins by the power of the Holy Ghost. In the book of Revelation, it speaks about the mark of the beast specifically and as well the seals of God. In Revelation 5:1 speaks of sea scrolls that have stay close until this appointed time. In chapter two of Revelation speaks of many seals of God. Revelation 9:4 tells a good reason to have God's seal upon your forehead. It will protect and separate you from those that will receive the wrath of God for not having His seal. This is like the blood on the door post when the Hebrew in Egypt was delivered from the death angel. The obedience to God's word with the blood on the doorpost seal them from the death angel. We are blood bought children of Christ. Revelation 20:3 tells of the seal that will be placed upon Satan, it will hold him for a little while for his end will be in the lake of fire, chain for eternity. I do not take God's seal lightly.

That's it for now. Thank you for your patient and time. Oh! Are there any questions? (Waiting.)

Man, Have Forgotten How to See

A faithless mind is a dangerous person.
Knowledgeless can leads to faithlessness.
The people perish from lack of knowledge;
A hopeless mind leads to bottomless despair.
Tossed by the wind, shifting with the waves
One fades through time.
Double minded is an unstable mind in all its ways
What I think affects what I see
I have forgotten how to see.
We are born in the gray;
Walking every day in dim sight
Spiritual clarity is impaired
It was after my deliverance I realized
I could have been spiritually bipolar and not aware.
Now I can see the imbalance in my world
It starts with me.
I must see the signs to tell the times.
I must see the reasons for these seasons.
I must see the Word fulfilled in my life.
Till the Light shows me the way.
A conversation leads to salvation.
The Light has arrived.
I have a choice to be alive
To see the grass greener
To see the present brighter.
A choice to stop deceiving myself
Though seeing I did not see.
Though hearing I did not understand.
I will be ever hearing but never understanding,
I will be ever seeing but never perceiving.
Come out of the darkness into the Light
I have forgotten how to see.
I no longer have friends, I had reached my end.
I have been trained to carry chains.
Day to day pressures have taken its toll
I rise, drained from the previous day strain.
I am tired of this way every day.
I want to be the true me; I want to be set free

I came up with a formula recipe; it sums the up like this.
Blood (grace + mercy) + believe + repentance (water & Spirit) = salvation
Salvation + (-iniquity) (blood) = suffering + denying self + obedience + (blood (-sin)).
Myself is a being, as one grain of sand
Abraham's fruits springing forth
Abraham's seeds growing faith.
I became one of those seeds
Numbers among the stars,
I once was a nobody, struggling,
Succeeding to become somebody in Christ Jesus,
The one from Nazareth.
What separated me from my Lord?
What did I go out into the desert to see?
Seeking a sign unable to see and
Looking for rest unable to find it,
I have been among an evil and adulterous generation.
Lord here am I, send me.
How can the blind lead the blind?
I had forgotten how to see; I have my Father in mind I know
No sign will be given except the sign of the prophet Jonah
If I do not see, how can I believe?
The world is a brighter place with Him.
Look where the Lord has brought me from,
Now I have my Father's eyes.
Amazing grace, once I had forgotten how to see.

Linda Bridges

Rapunzel

There was once a woman who became pregnant. She and her husband longed for a child. They were very much in love. One day she looked at a garden, a garden she had seen for years. She had a different feeling. She craved. In the garden, she was captivated by the plant, rapunzel. At the sight the woman's mouth watered. Unable to climb the fence she awaited her husband. When he got home, she immediately approaches him. The cravings lead her to passionately plead with him to get her a plant.

What was supposed to be a beautiful surprise turned into a crutch for the wife. She told him she was pregnant. They had long for a child but had very little and often put it off. The man understood little about craving for a pregnancy only that they could become severe. Her need for the plant sounded like life or death for her and the child. This left the husband in turmoil. He wondered what he should do. Love won.

Rapunzel is the name of a common delicious edible plant in the bellflower family. Once widely used as a salad for it leaves and roots. The leaves are like spinach, and it root is used like a radish. The plant itself is lovely. You have a beautiful spellbinding light blue or violet flower with bright green leaves. You can see why this plant would become fixate to the taste buds of a pregnant woman or was it curse. You don't just enjoy fresh green leaves but a crunchy root that will meet your nutritious need, Mm mm.

For a pregnant woman, this became addictive. There is weirder craving out there for pregnant women. Some of those weird cravings are anchovies, ice cubes, bath salt, sand and gravel, chewing sponges and toothbrush; I think you get the point. A rapunzel is the least of your craving problem for a pregnant woman unless your love one's welfare is at risk and you must steal them.

This sounds like Abraham looking at Sarah, because he knew the problem of sleeping with her handmaiden could cost. He could not deny her. The husband knew stealing from the garden could lead to problems, but he could not refuse his long awaited pregnant wife. Good thing he was a praying man. The Lord knows our actions affect us as well as our children. Through grace and mercy, he looks out for them. He understood the power of prayer and he needed divine intervention for his wife, him, and the unborn child. He did not expect to lose his child.

The husband sneaked into the garden at night. He stole a few rapunzels for his pregnant wife. It only calmed her for a few nights. The husband did not like where this was going. He was inexperienced with pregnant women. He knew this could get out of hand.

The husband knew stealing from the garden could lead to trouble. He did not know what else to do. He could not bring himself to refuse his crying wife. He sneaked again into the garden at night and stole more rapunzels. They did not last long. The next day she was out. As the cravings grew the rapunzels did not last long. She wanted more. The husband tried reasoning with his wife. He tried pleading with his wife to no avail. Then she stopped eating other food, obsessed with eating rapunzel. He went a fifth night.

The woman lived next door grew rapunzel and many other herbs in her garden. She was a medicine lady though some call her a witch. She had noticed the plants disappearance. She waited and caught the man this time. The Lady stepped out of the shadows. She said, "you are the one helping himself to my rapunzel." "Stealing is what you are doing." The husband said, "I am so sorry." He didn't deny it. He said to the medicine lady, "I have a pregnant wife who craves your rapunzels." He continued and said, "she stopped eating, she's crying all the time, and I don't know what to do." Now he told her, "my wife and unborn baby's life depend on eating rapunzel." He noticed the medicine lady did not seem surprise.

The medicine lady seethed an opportunity. She wanted a child. She propositioned the man, "get all you want but give me the baby at birth." At this request the man was torn in his heart. He knew he was dealing with a witch. She later said, "after the baby is wean".

The husband tried to reason with the witch. He said, "I would pay you even tend your garden." The husband being in despair did not want to lose both wife and child, finally agreed. He was then allowed to pick all the rapunzel for his wife's need. The witch made sure to give the wife not only rapunzel but other good herbs to help the pregnancy alone.

When the baby was born and weaned, the witch took the child. She left and raised the child as her own. She called the child, Rapunzel after the plant. The child eventually brought out good in the witch, but it did not last. The witch tried to spoil the child, she saw the child was too good to follow her steps in life. The witch tried to teach the child about herbs for selfish reasons but the child reasoned it out and used the knowledge for good. This made her more popular with the people. She had to talk the witch into allowing her to associate with other people. As the child got older she grew in innocence and beauty. She grew more beautiful with long curly hair. She attracted the attention of more people who saw her kindness and beauty. The witch saw where this was going and begin to plan. The witch did not like to share.

As her twelfth years' birthday approached the witch said, "we will do something special for your birthday." The witch told the child, "you cannot trust people these days, we must take precaution." The witch took Rapunzel to the woods on her twelfth-year birthday and put her in a prepared tower. She shut Rapunzel into the tower with one window then removed the door. She left an expansive room on top and one window for her, the witch, to come and go. There was a small window in the back. She bought supplies to Rapunzel weekly. When she was ready to go up into the tower she called, "Rapunzel let down your hair so I can climb up." Rapunzel being a good daughter always obeyed. This went on for several years.

One day out of the usual days Rapunzel was singing. A young man traveling through the woods heard her. He followed the singing to the tower. Later the young man who was a prince shouted up and said, "Lady in the tower, how goes your day." Rapunzel finally realized she was being called. Rapunzel looked out and said, "hello". The Prince found out that her name was Rapunzel. He was shocked by her beauty. Rapunzel did the forbidden she continues to talk to a stranger. The witch had warned her to be careful of stranger. The child who is now a lady was lonely. The witch never expected the girl to be found. The witch said to Rapunzel in the past, "this is for your own safety." She was to stay in the tower. Rapunzel was a dutiful daughter believed the witch until she talked to the Prince. Rapunzel remembered her kind neighbors and how they found her helpful. As Rapunzel and the young Prince became friend, he asked, "Can I come in?" Rapunzel was reluctant but she did not feel fear.

He had walked around the tower many times and did not see an opening. He asked, "Rapunzel how does one enter." Rapunzel invited him in and said, "I have to let down my hair." She told him, "climb up." He did.

Rapunzel and the Prince became close. One-day he asked Rapunzel, "will you marry me." She happily said, "yes". The Prince told her about people. He told her about his home, but he did not tell her he was a prince. They talked about having children one day. They talked about helping other less fortunate. The Prince talked about diverse cultures, animals, plants, and many amazing things in the world. He wanted to show it all to her. He also gave her interesting gifts. Those she hid. She developed a desire to wander. The Prince saw the trap she was in. He knew to hide from the witch, she was coming and going.

The Prince said, "Rapunzel I will get you out of this prison." Rapunzel did not know what to say, finding out she was in a prison was unspeakable. The Prince asked, "give me time to plan." Until then he said, "I will bring you threads of silk." She used the silk to make a rope. Rapunzel said, "I know how to thread and plait." She lovingly and patiently did her hair often. She had little else to do, and it took time.

Rapunzel made plans to steal away with the Prince early one night. The witch will make her usual stop. Today Rapunzel was so thrilled she forgot to hide her silk. She had packed a few things she wanted to take. There wasn't many. The witch came up as usually and left her supplies. The witch said, "hello Love, how are you feeling today?" She noticed Rapunzel was more cheerful than usually. That was fine with her. Rapunzel said, "good, and thank you for the books." The witch did not want to lose Rapunzel. Keeping Rapunzel locked up and fed made the selfish witch feel important. As the witch grew closer to leaving she noticed items were missing out of the room. As she was about to climb down Rapunzel's hair she saw the silk. The witch knew instantly someone was visiting Rapunzel. Not only visiting but preparing her to leave. The witch saw red. She was furious. The witch climbs back in the window and said, "ungrateful child you will not leave me." The witch grabbed Rapunzel, who did not know what to do. With scissor in hand she began to cut Rapunzel's hair. Rapunzel saw her life flash before her eyes and the thoughts of not seeing the prince made her furious, "no, no, no," she screamed. The witch grabbed Rapunzel and the silk. She threw the silk out the window, and down her and Rapunzel went. She did not stop until she deposits Rapunzel far into the wilderness. She left her there.

The witch came back to the tower, furious at who was taking her Rapunzel. She waited. The Prince did his walk around the tower. After making sure he did not see the witch He called, "Rapunzel let down your long golden hair." The hair came down. The Prince climbed up and to his surprise he saw the witch. She began to wave her arms and hands to throw powder on him. He knew without a doubt nothing good will come from that except poison or a curse. He immediately saw Rapunzel was not there. He tries to ask, "where's Rapunzel?" There was no reasoning with the witch. The Prince ran for the window and grabbed Rapunzel's hair with the silk tangled in. He leaped out the window, grabbing thorns to break his fall. The thorns tore into him and his eyes. His eyes were scratch and immediately began to bleed. His heart was on Rapunzel and his next hold to keep from falling to his death.

Rapunzel was found by a hunter who took her to his village. The woman of the village took care of her. They saw she had skills and was not afraid to work. Rapunzel was sad, but the village taught her how to pray and to keep her hope alive. Rapunzel could style hair, sew, and her use of herbs made her very helpful in the village.

The Prince got away. He wandered for years, living on the mercy of others. Invisibly he was lead through deserted lands and wilderness. Mostly blind, he increased his prayer life one day at a time. One day he heard singing. He recognized the voice. He made his way to the voice. It was his Rapunzel. They gave thanks to the Lord that the Prince had told Rapunzel about they were made whole. They embraced and gave thanks to the Lord as many tears fell from Rapunzel's eyes onto the Prince face. Perfect peace came to Rapunzel and sight to the Prince. The Prince immediately headed home with Rapunzel. They were married and live happily ever after.

What happen to the witch? She had no way to climb down. It's believed she is trapped in the tower that she built. When you dig, a ditch, digs two, because the first one is for you

THE END

Sleeping Beauty

Once upon a time there was a fair lady. She did not have much, but what she did have she used it wisely. She was well liked in her neighborhood. Many recognized the light within her. At an early age, she received the Lord. She readily had a smile for people, kind words, or just being her present self. She liked people. Being a peoples' person, she did not meet many strangers.

As the young girl grew she took her skills very seriously. Her mother being a wise and virtuous woman had many talks with her about life. She taught her how to live life productively. She learned early about the Lord without many distractions. Mom rarely allowed outside influences in the house and only certain games were allowed. She knew that making the right choices kept Christ in her life. She prayed daily and loved singing her favorite praise songs to the Lord. Many admired her heavenly voice. She grew up to be a fair lady. She lived life with a positive attitude and shunned confusion. She did not notice the resentment aim at her from a small lady.

The small Lady path crossed often with the fair Lady. The fair Lady was always going somewhere with a purpose. She loved working with children. The small Lady grumbled one day and said, "that child is spoiled, spoiled rotten; she looked like she does not have a care in the world," and she walked on.

One day the fair Lady accidentally bumped the small Lady and knocked over her bags; the small Lady grumbled. The fair Lady helped her pick the bags up with an apology. The fair Lady said, "I am so sorry, I must slow down." She continued to help the small Lady pick up her packages. The small Lady grumbled with a "hmm mp," and walked away. The fair Lady did not know what to make of that because she was ready to apologize again. She realized she was late and took off, forgetting about the incident.

Then one day she saw the small Lady walking in the rain. The fair Lady remembered the small Lady and shared her umbrella. The fair Lady spoke, "what a wet day." The small Lady grumbled, "hmm mph." The fair Lady got the small Lady to where she was going and told her, "have a good day."

One day a King was riding his horse. He almost ran the small Lady over but curved in time. He jumped off the horse to apologize and make sure she was well. The small Lady slapped at his hand and pointed her finger at him then she grumbled.

The small Lady came from a village of small people. She was the tallest in her village and the smallest in this town. She was taught to be silent and respect her elder. Because she was different she was criticized often so she hid in her work. She stopped trying to socialize and did her job. Her job was important but she got no respect. Someone had to do the job. She was too big at home in her village and to little outside home. She seemed to unintentionally intimidate her elders so they sent her away. This caused unintentionally offense. She was looked over in town and had hope for things to be better, but they took her for granted. It made it difficult for her to make friends. Even though she was a difficult person, but not intentionally. If they only knew who she really was.

One day the small Lady decided to meet with the town Mayor so they would know her work in the town. She thought, "if they knew what I did maybe I will get my recognition." The small Lady grumbled with a smile and said, "I would not know what to say, but this is my chance; I will think of something".

Things did not turn out the way it should. The secretary introduced her to the Mayor. The small Lady tried to talk. The Mayor kept talking to the secretary as if she did all the work and left the small Lady out. The secretory did not try to correct the Mayor. The small Lady gave up, walking behind them grumbling. She turned around and left. The Mayor asked the secretary, "how was the work accomplish." The secretary turned around and said, "Madam could you explain." They both noticed she was gone. They realized they were rude but like the others, they did nothing to correct it.

The small Lady's job was important but she got no respect. Someone had to do the job. The small Lady endured the loneliness; she did not cut her duties and expected the same from other. People that worked around her did not like her but she was fair and kept a tight crew. People's health depended on it. She knew unless she purchases the powder and prep it up to the correct strength there could be death. She placed the powder in the water, neutralizing it, then it ran out of the factory. The water from the village would be deadly if not neutralized. Finally, the factory closed and the water no longer posed a threat to the town. The job of the small Lady was no longer needed. The small Lady retired early and decided to stay in the kingdom.

The small Lady never grew in standard though her appearance was lovely. The small attention she received she declined or ignored because she never got over her low self-esteem. The small Lady began to seek solitude she thought this is what I want. But when she went outside she felt like she was missing something.

As the fair Lady grew up in grace and beauty, she caught the attention of the King. He fell in love with the fair Lady. She was courted by the King and they were married. After several years of marriage, the fair Lady, oh I meant the Queen became pregnant. It seemed their union was going to be complete. The King and Queen will have their child.

The child came into the world as children do just like a ray of sunshine. After the christening of the King and Queen only child a gathering was held. The town people was invited, along with everyone throughout the country came to the palace. Seven elders were asked to be her God mothers from the village. Each Elder had a gift. The Elders came forward offering their special gift through prayer. First Elder blessed her to live the living word so its beauty would shine inside as well as out. Second Elder blessed her with knowledge. Third Elder blessed her with grace. The Fourth Elder blessed her with dance. The Fifth Elder blessed her with song. The Sixth Elder blessed her with music. As the King and Queen listened to the blessings they could not wait until the last. They knew the best was save for the last.

As the Seventh Elder approached, she stops. The room became quiet.

The small Lady had not been seen for a while. She was thought to have left the kingdom. The small Lady grumbled, "enough is enough I am an important Elder of this community; I am not dead." She came to the front grumbling. Aging had not been kind to her; a life of resentment, unforgiveness, and grumbling had taken its toll on her.

The small Lady was the Eight Elder. She was angry; very angry because she thought she was not invited to the christening. She came forward walking with years of bitterness, grievance, and resentment from getting no respect. The grudge she felt for the couple bypassed the Hatfield and McCoy Feud. She saw in them a life that passed her by and they were somehow to blame. She focused all this ill will toward the innocent child. She grumbled, "let them taste life with the child and then let it be scratched away." She began to speak evil on the child. The small Lady said, "she will be pricked on her finger by a spindle of a spinning wheel and die!" Upon the last word, the small Lady turned around and left. The King and Queen tried to explain but they were not given time.

The crowd was troubled. They grew loud. They grew silent as the Seventh Elder approached. The Seventh Elder came forward calmly. She had not given her gift. She knew a prayer to counter the curse. The Mother, the Queen, was a praying woman, she held on to faith. The King lacked faith. The six Elders stood in agreement standing on faith.

The King became furious and the Queen tried to calm him. If only the King believed like the Queen. He was not a bad King. The Seventh Elder murmur, "Yea of little faith. Have faith." He started to feed the curse. He ordered all spindle to be remove from the land. This lead all the Elder to try and explain to the King that the curse had no more power than he gave it. The King was frightened and said, "my child; immediately remove all spindle from the land and they are not to return. The King said loudly, "this is a royal decree."

The Seventh Elder knew the power of prayer as she got everyone attention she spoke, "the prayer of righteous availed much." She prayed to remove the evil curse. Instead of dying, she prophesied, "the Princess will fall into a deep sleep for 100 years and awaken to love." The Seventh Elder knew there may be a problem with the family's separation. She knew more prayer was needed. She decided to put the kingdom to sleep. The Elder knew the importance of moving in the will of God. The seventh Elder extended her blessing to the eight Elder and spoke, "love that cover a multitude of faults shall find it way to the eight Elder despite the aughts."

The Elder knew that the King and Queen were kind, but sometimes you can offend a person unaware. Trouble will find you. It was good to have the living God on your side. The King tried to remove all spindle from the country. In his loving fatherly way, he tried to help God.

The King was a God-fearing man but we must have learned what happen to us when we help God but not obey God. Emotions get to roiling. Good intentions well-meant looked good but will accomplish nothing and many times the end thereof is death. You need divine intervention and obedience because you just made a simple situation worse.

Faith was put to the test. Ye of little faith. What is death to our Lord? He took the sting from death, the certainty from death, and the eligibility from death. It has no claim on his people. We sleep we are not dead. There is no finality in death for those that believe in the living word, He is risen. The princess will be raised in the living word. The worldly King in his moment of panic forgot this. The Queen did not. The Elders did not. The Queen believed in her Lord, for he is Alpha and Omega, the Beginning and End. She knew the Lord is the past, now, and future. He changed not. He would hear their cry, their prayers, they acknowledgment of Him, and He will have blessed them to prevail.

The Queen knew divine intervention was needed. In her heart she called out to the Lord to save her child. She was going on a three day fast and asked the people to join her. As time pass the King was depressed then the Queen step up to keep the nation moving with no time to consult her husband. She ruled the inner court as necessary. The Queen said, "I and my handmaiden will fast along with anyone that was sincere and willing. I will tell the Lord of Lords that I will stand in the gap not only for my child but for my country and if I perish then I perish."

Lack of faith was noted from the King. The Queen was determined not to let one bad apple (situation) destroy the kingdom. Grace and mercy abound. She knew her husband was a good man; she girdled him up in the Word. He could not help but be affected in a positive way by the living word. He came out of his depression and resume his mantle. He had hope but he did not allow the spindle to return. He would see out the trials ahead. The Queen knew in the outcome faith will be establish. By faith victory would be theirs.

In the meantime, the King and Queen sent messengers to the Eight Elder. They did not let the false accusations go unanswered. They sent apologies and gifts to the small Lady. They had her research and realized her position in the community for many years was essential. They realized that no recognition was given to her for her sacrifices she made on her job to the kingdom.

They also found about the pollutants the factory spew in the water before they secretly called the small Lady to come in and clean up their mess. Though the factory was close they were fined and judged for endangering the environment as well as the people's health.

As the Queen prayed and was led by the Lord to visit the small Lady. It was then she knew they had met before. Sheepishly she met with the small Lady and they talked. The small Lady remembered the Queen as a child. She thought, "always scurrying about."

The Queen was awkward around her and she realize it was her standard as an Elder that intimidated the Queen. The small Lady knew that the fair Lady, the Queen, was sincere when she apologized as a child, and allowed her to use her umbrella and regretted knocking her bags down. She was moved by the Queen's respect. As they talked the small Lady realized she misunderstood the Queen. The small Lady asked, "forgive my impulsive nature." The Queen did.

The small Lady knew she could not undo the curse so she prayed to the Lord. She started it off with repentance and forgiveness as she forgave those who had hurt her. And then she prayed that the Lord would bridle her tongue and please intervene on her foolish curse.

Time passed. Around sixteen years later the princess was a ball of energy. Playing in the palace she saw a door open that usually is close. Curiosity got the best of her and she went in. She came upon an old lady peddling a spinning wheel that reminded the princess of her toys. The princess did not know what she was seeing. She was never told not to touch one. Everyone in the kingdom was forbidden by law to have one so she had never seemed one. The princess did not know this or why. Curiosity carried her further into the room. She asked, "what is it?" The old lady was happy to explain, "this is a spindle, see how it spins?"

The small Lady knew the curse had to come to pass and she had to reap what she had sowed. She had to bring in a spindle to cause the lovely child harmed. This caused her to hurt along with the family and she knew it was only fair. She accepted her fate, her part in the curse. The small Lady and her disguise work all too well. She was ready to sleep with the family also.

The old lady loved the spinning of the wheel. Her mind did not remember the curse so there will be no change of heart. When the princess asked, "can I spin?" The old lady was happy to share. What the worst she could do she thought, "prick her finger. It will heal."

The child pricked her finger and immediately fell asleep as if she was dead. The old lady said, "wake up child". She could not understand what was happening. She said, "Oh my, I will get help."

The King and Queen were called. They held each other and their faith. The child looked asleep. She was softly breathing and her pulse was faint. They had hope for this moment never to come. They called for the Seventh Elder. She confirmed the cursed was active and prayer was being answer. The child was sleeping.

The King and Queen had the child moved to a private room upstairs and closed. The Elder saw the distress on the King, Queen, and the people. She knew it was time for all to sleep. She had the King and Queen to sit on their throne and talk. They were not aware, but immediately all went to sleep. As the upper room was seal, so was the kingdom. Prayers were being answered, they would sleep together and awake together. Most importantly there would be peace and the love would flow in the land. They would be saved from what was meant for their bad by it being turned for their good.

The Lord worked in mysterious ways and in wonder to be performed. There was nothing too hard for the Lord. Brambles and thorns grew around the palace. The kingdom became surrounded by a wilderness, shielding it from the outside world. The princess slept on. The princess was not disturbed.

Once the Lord closed a door it is closed and when he opens the door it remains open. This is done only to the chosen individuals. Many times, animals and people walked through the forest and did not notice the kingdom.

As time passed and ordered is kept, evil will attempt to usurps that which is good and right. The evil that presided over the curse was not happy that the child slept peacefully. After fifty years past the evil grew frustrated. It called an ancient dragon to destroy the village as the people slept.

The evil had addressed the watcher on occasions. The evil tried to bring the watcher to his way of thinking. Such as let end this so we can be about another duty. How boring can it be? Do you really want to do this for a hundred years? The watcher stays sober and vigilant.

The prayers were sent and requested to the only God that never slept nor slumber. He saw the evil stirring, plotting against His will. The watcher was given the duty to observe and keep the peace while time past. Little did he know that the peace was to be tested.

With the aid of the evil combined with the dragon its appeared out of the clouds instantly. It charged the village with fiery darts spewing out of its mouth. The village was not harmed because the fire did not penetrate. And the dragon tried again. It flew toward the village to rip it apart with talons and teeth. Upon reaching the village, about to touch it the dragon passed through the village and it appeared where it was before.

The dragon shook the evil off and looked. He really looked. There was a light stirring. The light stirred fear in the dragon. There were no people moving about. The dragon being and old creature, but not a fool, felt fear. He knew if he attacked this time there will be no coming back. He fled. The evil in its' rage charged the Light and was consumed. Peace returned and the village slept on.

One day a hunter that was a prince, a man after God's own heart, came through the woods. He had hunted these woods as a child. He followed the stag's tracks and they disappeared at one of his favorite spot. This day was difference. He noticed buildings and saw it was a big building surrounded by smaller building. As he approached he realized it was a palace. The prince thought, "how can something so big be hidden all this time." He knew something supernatural was at work. He girdled up his integrity, stood strong and tall in his courage. He dared not turn around; he did not think he could find this place again. He braced himself even more when he saw the brambles and thorns. "This will take some work but something worthwhile is better when earned," murmur the hunter. Jewelry, books, artifacts that he knew he would fine had his heart racing. The prince knew something precious and worthwhile awaited him. He looked up toward the hill in his Spirit for direction. He knew he could do all through Christ Jesus that strengthens him. His foot moves forward.

He could not resist entering the bushes. He was ready to fight his way through. He knew he might be ripped to shreds. Just when it got impossible. Behold! A path appeared and he could walk through the brambles and thorns into the village without harm. He stepped onto the path and through the front door of the palace.

He saw people asleep. They looked like they stopped where they were and took a nap. He went through the front door of the palace. He saw the King and Queen asleep. The path took him upstairs to a door. He opened the door and behold there was beauty asleep. Sleeping Beauty. He knew some thought he was a hopeless romantic. Right now, he knew how Solomon felt. In the book of Solomon his mind went to chapter 1:2; the prince said, "Let him kiss me with the kisses of his mouth." The love was instant. He kissed the princess on the lip and she immediately awaken. The Princess was just as attractive to the prince. The kingdom awakened and went about their tasks. The King and Queen awakened also. The prince told the story to the princess that had been circulating for years. About a princess that was cursed to sleep for a hundred years and how it came about.

The princess who had slept in peace found her parents. She introduced the prince to her parents. A meal was prepared. After dining and walking the prince ask for the princess' hand in marriage she agreed. The King and Queen look around and saw all was well. They knew God is the only true God and he is real.

THE END

Little Red

The world is full of Little Reds; we find this Little Red with earplugs in her ears. Music blasting! Mother was about to send Little Red on a simple errand. Mother was selective about what she hears. So, she heard about the Big Bad Wolf on the move.

Mother heard about it from the neighbors. Little Red was texting. She missed it. Mother heard about it again on the radio. Little Red was practicing new moves. She missed it. Mother heard it again on television and called Little Red to watch. Mother said, "Little Red come see what roaming the country side." Little Red said, "coming". She came but when Mother step out. Little Red put on the games. And yes, she missed it.

Mother told Little Red, "take the plugs out of your ears and remember there is danger in the woods." She encouraged Little Red to listen. Little Red did. Mother did not take her eyes off Little Red. Mother explained, "Little Red, Granny is sick." Little Red was concern about Granny. No one could cook an apple pie like Granny. No one would keep her cats like Granny. She asked, "is it was bad." Little Red knew Granny was not getting younger. She knew she needed the proper herbs and grubs (food). "She be back up on her feet soon," Mother said, "no., I don't think it bad" Little Red was hungry so she tuned the rest out. She heard her phone beep and could barely wait to answer. She did not hear about the Big Bad Wolf and his tricks. Everything she needed to know she was told but she did not listen. She missed it.

She remembered at the last moment her red coat, that Granny made for her. Little Red loved her Granny.

Mother told, "Little Red take this basket of food and herbs for Granny and do not talk strangers! Do not leave the path!" She said, "Little Red traveled while it is day and don't dillies dally." Finally, she said, "do not eat Granny's food." Mother prayed and blessed the food, blessed Little Red, blessed Granny, and sent Little Red on her way.

As Little Red left the house humming, she saw wildflowers and picked a bunch for Granny. As she neared the woods Little Red put the earplug in her ears. As she got closer to the fresh smelling green forest she missed the watching eyes. The eyes followed her on the path. Soon her earplugs stopped receiving in the dead zone of the woods. She took them out. Thank God. Just in the nick of time. She heard noisy footsteps. She looked around and saw a well-groomed but big dog wagging his tail.

The wolf got tired of waiting. The wolf was hungry. He was going to try for chicken that night from the village, but he noticed Little Red. He watched, hoping the girl would leave the path. That would make his work easier. The wolf did not want pesky neighbors to see him on the path. The wolf kept up with the news too. He knew hunters were on the watch for him. Because of the wolf killings the hunters were given permission to down size the wolf population. The wolf knew he was the bad apple. The wolf knew not to let his stomach rush him into mistakes as so many times before. The mistake could lead to the end of him. He knew the truth. He was not ready to stop the flow of destruction, killing, and stealth. The thrill kept him going. He would never tire of it. He didn't bother to tiptoe through the forest because the girl (get this) had earplugs on. 'Ha Ha Ha," laugh the wolf. The wolf said to himself, "could this get any simpler? I was going to snatch the child. I would make it quick." Then the girl took the earplugs off," The wolf said to himself, "I must move with caution." Then she started cooing to me. "I going to work with that," said the wolf and wagged his tail.

The big dog wagged his tail and approached Little Red. Little Red said, "coo coo" and puppy talked to the wolf. Oh! I meant the dog. When the dog began to speak to Little Red she wasn't surprise.

The games, shows, and music she listened too taught her to expect these things. She accepted them as they come. Go with the flow you won't live forever. Enjoy life in its grand moments. Until the day comes and she realized this will not work.

It was a blessing Little Red had a praying Mother. And our God sit high and look low. He knew that wolf would be a wolf. He saw Little Red in her favorite coat and knew her head was in the clouds. The Lord heard Mom's prayers in glory and activated it. They went into effect. Windows were open to pour blessings upon the child; that she was not aware that she needed. Extra angels were sent to help the guardian angel. Overtime did the child work the angel! Thank God, our children are under the promise. We are wise to thank God for our children and give them back to him. The anointing is upon them through our faithfulness in the Lord through the living word in our life. We are blessed and our children are blessed.

The wolf-dog introduced himself (not as a wolf). The dog said, "hello little one." He wasted no time getting all into the girl's business. She held nothing back.

Little Red forgot and disobeyed rule one. Do not talk to strangers. The dog could talk and it was a stranger. The dog fell into step with Little Red. The dog said, "I'm going that way, do you want to share that basket?" Little Red said, "no, it's for granny she is sick." The wolf thought that name sound familiar.

Before the sun moved past noon, Little Red told the dog that she was on her way to her Granny's house. She was bedridden not feeling well. She had some food for her. She then began to complain about her cell phone not working, no music, hot, thirsty, and just bored.

The dog was tired of Little Red's complaining, but managed to keep smiling. She asked, "could you finish the walk with me; it is boring by myself." The dog looked up beside Little Red head with delight thinking you will not have to worry about that much longer.

They walked down the road. Little Red groomed the dog, picked at his ears, scratched his head, and the wolf was tired. The wolf did not know how much more he could take.

The wolf first saw Little Red. He realized she was not very big. She looked plumper from a distance. It was good news she told him about her Granny being bedridden. The wolf cheered up. The dog looked Little Red up and down and said, "that's a lovely coat." But he was sizing her up. The wolf decided to bid his time. Little Red was a small morsel one meal; he could wait on an upgrade. Two for one, one could not put a fight. Like taking candy from a baby. Knocked down two birds with one stone. The wolf was happy he was not going hungry tonight.

Little Red said, "my granny made it for me; she knows I love red." Little Red told the dog that granny said, "it gets cool in the woods and the coat will keep me warm."

As they walked down the path the dog saw a figure in the woods, knowing he's being hunted. His reputation preceded him. He zoomed his sight in and realized it was a familiar figure. It was the huntsman. He was walking straight toward the huntsman. He feared the huntsman. "I got to get off this path," the wolf thought. He did what he does best, he lied to the child. He said, "I know a shortcut let leave the path." Little Red agreed and without waiting for the girl he took off. He quickly wanted to get out of sight; he forgot the girl for a moment. He left her behind.

Little Red was trying to follow, but could not, she said, "I'm getting tired." The dog led the way and made detour. The trees branches and brambles were thick. She tripped, stumbled, and spilled the basket. She put the items back in the basket. Little Red said, "wait, I've I torn my coat." When her coat was torn, she said aloud "darn." She traced her steps back to the path. Her stepped became smooth and straight forward. She also realized on this path; she knew where she was going. She began to think, "What was I thinking following a stranger?"

It goes to show; they may stray but they come back. Little Red steps were prayed to remain on the path.

Little Red finally saw the huntsman and waved. She knew the huntsman from the neighborhood. She approached the huntsman and said, "hello, I'm going to granny's house." She told the huntsman that her Granny was sick.

The huntsman said, "hurry to Granny house, you are cutting it close to dark." Little Red said, "it is; I did not know it was this late."

It could get dark early in the forest, but he knew she knew this. Little Red had made this trip many times. The huntsman said, "if you go straight to Granny's house you will get there before dark." Little Red skipped off feeling very elevated with joy and happiness. She was going to see Granny. She almost forgot. She asked," have you seen a big dog?" If she had that dog it would complete her happiness so she thought. Little Red wanted a dog.

The huntsman looked confused, and was about to shrug it off when the light hit him. He told Little Red, "I have not seen a dog."

The huntsman knew the woods, too. He decided to whine up this job so he could visit his dear friend Granny and Little Red.

The wolf knew of Granny's house but would not go there on his own again. The little woman looked weak and feeble, but she was quick with her wit. He remembered the time he thought he would rest by her chicken coop. He saw Granny on the other side of the house. Before he got to the opposite side by the chicken coop, Granny was there with a pitch fork. Of all things, beware of the Grannies. Granny, while on her feet and in good health was a force to be reckoned with in the Lord. Granny had a hedge around her property. It was time consuming and dangerous to get on that property; but Little Red had given him the info he needed. Now Granny was ill, bedridden, she was due a visit.

As the wolf approached Granny's house, he walked around the property to see what was lacking and found the house had developed a few cracks. The wolf was swift, but was tired. He was tired of walking around dry places. He thought to himself after my snack I will clean up and rest. Take a napped before Little Red gets her.

The wolf reflected when he ran with a pack. They left him behind and claimed he was slow. He caused many accidents and got himself hurt because he would not work with the pack. They were angry with him and his tricks. Many innocent wolves were killed because of his tactics. To a huntsman a wolf looked like a wolf. He figures he would show them the pack up.

The wolf came up to the door and tried the knob, it was locked. The wolf knocked on the door. No answer. The wolf knocked harder, and was persistence until he heard a weak voice say. "Who is it?" said granny. The wolf cleared his throat and said, "it's me Granny."

Granny was sick but not deaf. She thought to herself that the voice did not sound like a voice she knew. Granny asked again, "Who is it?"

The wolf realizing, he was not fooling any one answered differently in a small voice "Granny I love my red coat." There was only one person she made a red coat for so she gave permission and said, "come inside dear."

The wolf tested the door knob, it opened. He went inside. Granny was getting up to greet her Little Red when she saw the wolf enter. Granny screamed, "Lord Jesus." She ran toward the kitchen grabbed her best biggest cutting knife and thought, "I going to get wolf blood on my carving knife. Oh, well." She thrusted the thought aside. Then she felt something snag her nice nightgown. She wondered did she have the color thread to fix it with a needle. When she turned around and realized it was the wolf she was furious at the spots it was leaving on the floor. Just when she thought enough was enough. She turned around to stab the wolf. She tripped and hit her head on the kitchen sink. The knife flew out of her hand. The wolf said, "whew! That was close!!!" Down went Granny to the floor. The wolf whisper, "she unconscious." The wolf thought this was too easy and was about to clamp down on Granny when he heard whistling.

Little Red made good time with the blessing of being obedience and staying on the path.

The wolf grabbed Granny and threw her into the closet. The wolf said, "my second snack; I don't want to scare her off." He saw other night gowns and caps. He grabbed one set and put them on. The wolf smiled and said, "this will do."

Meantime the huntsman was caught up in his work. He was chopping wood and about to prepare dinner when he heard a soft voice saying, "Little Red". THEN he remembered. He immediately stopped what he was doing, grabbed his ax and ran to Granny's house. It came back to his remembrance. He must ask Little Red about the big dog.

As Little Red got closer to Granny's house she felt peaceful, safe, and in need of sweets. Granny always had what she needed.

Little Red wiped off her shoes, knocked on the door. A scratchy voice said come in. To Little Red it sounded like she got a sick throat. Little Red skipped and bounced into the house. She was ready to pounce on Granny with hugs and kisses, but she did not want Granny's cold. When she noticed, illness did not agree with Granny. There was something sticking out of her head. Could she have fallen? Little Red thought, "your eyes are so big granny your blood pressure must be up!" And those teeth! Was she brushing? Little Red was a curious child wanted to find out before she approached the bed. Little Red questioned," Granny what big ears you have?" Wolf-Granny answered, "better to hear you with my dear." (Little Red thought to herself well I let that past). Little Red asked, "Granny what big eyes you have?" Wolf-Granny answered, "Better to see you with my dear." As the Wolf-Granny hoped she will come closer.

Little Red thought those eyes were big, but she was a child what did she know? Little Red said, "Granny what big teeth you have--." Before Little Red could finish the sentence, the wolf finished it. The wolf remembered this child could talk all day, and he would be at this all night. He was hungry. He jumped out of the bed shouting, "the better to eat you with my dear."

It took no time for Little Red to move out of the direction of the big dog. Now she realized it is a WOLF! Little Red dodged the wolf which was difficult in the house. She was up too it, warm up from skipping to the house. While she was running through the house she saw Granny's knife. She scooped it up and continued to dodge the wolf. Little Red was terrified but she managed to keep her wits about her while she barely stayed out of the wolf's teeth. The wolf tired, hungry, and ready to put an end to this. He began to wonder could it be possible that his friends were right about him. The wolf readied himself, gather the strength for a great leap.

Little Red was tired and terrified; she knew her leg were about to give out. She didn't understand how she lasted this long. She kept an eye on the wolf. She decided it was time to end this. She turned around and knew the wolf was about to leaped. By faith she stretched out her hands with the knife pointed out.

The wolf saw small and helpless Little Red as his meal at last. Then in his powerful leap (that impressed even himself) he saw that the girl had a knife! He could not stop his leap. True to his strength and direction he landed on Little Red. But the knife got him first. "There still a chance to get one bite in," the wolf thought.

After Little Red stopped screaming and realized she was alive. She opened her eyes and stared the wolf in the face and said, "oh no." He was grinning and opening his mouth with those big teeth when his head went rolling toward the kitchen.

The huntsman came quickly to Granny's house and upon approaching. He heard the screams. The huntsman moved faster! He bust through the door upon seeing the wolf on the child did not hesitate to cut off the wolf's head.

When Little Red saw the head of the wolf roll, she then noticed the huntsman standing in Granny's house. They did not see Granny and thought the worst. The huntsman asked, "did I get here in time?" The huntsman and Little Red looked around for Granny. Little Red with had tears falling down her face and said, "I do not see here." They did not see Granny. The huntsman was about to open the wolf up to search for Granny, that turned out to be unnecessary. The huntsman and Little Red could hear stomping and fussing in the closet. Low and behold when they opened the door. It was Granny. Granny came out of the closet swinging her fist left and right. She was not going down without a fight. She said a choice words that I cannot write. She stated, "I will choke that wolf to death with my last breath." "He should give up something to take something." She farther said, "I am going to give him the indigestion of death; I just wish I had my knife to gut him from top to bottom."

Finally, Granny heard talking. She realized her neighbor, the huntsman, was in her house trying to calm her and Little Red. She asked, "are we safe." They said, "the bad wolf is dead."

Little Red was overfilled with joy. She gave Granny her best hugs and kisses. She ran and grabbed the basket of grub for Granny. She had thrown them at the wolf but they were still in the basket. She realized later she lost her earplugs but she didn't care. She began to realize that part of life was about survival. Family! She needed to start paying attention.

Granny thanked the huntsman and invited him to come back for coffee sometime. Little Red spent the night with Granny. The huntsman took the wolf with him.

Little Red thought she helped save Granny's life. Then she knew she was the cause of the wolf coming to Granny's house. Little Red thought I hope Mom do not learn about this. She was right about not talking to stranger. Little Red remembered the looks on the huntsman and Granny face and knew her Mom would find out. Little hope in that, I tell Mom the first chance I get. Better me than latter. Then she asked, "Granny do you have any pie."

Never trust a stranger-friend;
No one Knows how it will end
As you are pretty, so be wise,
Wolves may lurk in every guise.

by Lisinka

Little Red learned to set aside her earplugs. She learned the importance of a time out. She learned she like helping other. She began to keep up with news alerts and reading a daily word. She did not let electronics take over her life again. She also became a huntswoman and was very good at it.

THE END

Go Fish, Fisherman Of Man

You gave your child a fish. He asked for ketchup. You gave your child ketchup. He realized the fries were missing. You tell him though ketchup taste wonderful on food chain, you can live without it. Don't be a creature of habit. Habits can be broken. Most habits need to be broken.

You are home late again with a supper you scraped up. Taste pretty good though.

Your child is in his own world ask for a pop. Before you can grab the pop, he is holding his throat. He wants to breathe. You realize he is choking; he is choking on a bone.

You don't panic. Well, you try not to panic. He wants you to remove the bone. He is pointing in his mouth. No problem. He motions for you to reach down his throat to remove the object. His eyes search your eyes; plead with your eyes to fix the problem. He sees the calmness in your eyes and stays calm. In your eyes reflect your faith; in your heart, you are praying away the problem.

He's still not breathing well. You have had this problem before and since. It not as often and he is growing out of it.

When he was born, the room was full of people. You were told there were one midwife and one nurse. You know now the others were angels. Because you saw the room full of people. Messengers and one carried the breath from God for your baby. You know he has a special anointing from the Lord. God knew you would need. You saw them lift up your baby, he was blue. The pregnancy was not difficult. The midwife laid the baby down and shook her head. One of the nurses in the room picked the baby up and rocked him. His color returned and he started to cry. She brought me my baby. The mid wife rushed back in to the cradle but the baby was in my arms. She looks confused. I began to feed my baby. That was our simple beginning. There was always us; Jesus, baby, and me.

You've had dreams; you've prayed you've waited in anticipation to hold your baby. You were told not to have him; you were told there will be difficulties. But you kept the faith. You've known personally from dust we came and dust we will go back too. You've had to learn that recently. Your baby was all you had left of your family. He was the sum of your family, your hope, and your fruit. You knew it was a boy. You knew a lot of things.

Our breaths by breath come from the breath of God. He giveth and He taketh. Today He gives a breath. The baby is on the receiving end. What God starts He finish. As God breathe out. We breathe in. God's lungs are our air reservoir. God's lungs are our air purification system.

The baby breathed! Peace settles in the room. You know you must tell him.

The Bone is removed.

Your child wants to finish the fish. You throw away the bone from his throat. You tell him he can finish it, it's ok to eat please be carefully. Fall off the horse get back on. The child asks for a napkin to clean the grease off his hands. You give him a napkin, after his hands are clean. He asked to play games in your book. You let him.

(I think back to my childhood when the family ate fish. At an early age me and my sibling ate fish with bones, lot of bones, safely. I remembered my baby brother going through the growing stage to eat fish. There was so many of us that food was not wasted. You did not leave meat on the bones to speak frankly. We learned early to remove the bones from the fish.

My baby brother got strangle on a fish bone. It happened from time to time and Mom would hit us in the back and we spit it out or give us a piece of light bread then we will swallow it down. She kept up regular with castor oil or cod liver oil, now I know it came out.

This time my baby brother was having serious problems and Mom kept watching him. She finally came over and reach into his mouth with her finger hook. She seemed to grab something and it must have been the fish bone. Then he coughed, gagged, and spit. He got his breath and continue eating more cautiously. He is one of the ministers in our family.

I also notice children with calling (anointing) on their lives are harder to raise without a close walk with Jesus. It does not mean they are rebellious or bad with emphasis, because they grow up like other children. They still go through their stages of life too. But the outside forces try to take them out early is heavy. It is active in trying to destroy their lives (them) early. The pressure is really on the parents. If the parents are not anointed or praying parents they will become worse parents with good intentions or just bad parents. Bad parents that wake up one day and wonder why they did not do better and the Lord will have to deliver them from guilt. The enemy used them to destroy their own children. Not always with death. Criticism, abuse, doubt, and many negative ways or spirits they inflict on the child. You see doubt itself have destroy many dreams then failure ever can. If there is no self-esteem, hope, and belief in nothing (they fall for anything), then the child is faithless, hopeless, and spiritually dead. And the parent is in despair wondering what went wrong. Jesus is the answer.)

As the child multitasks himself sleepy, he asks for a bedtime story. You bath him as you tell him his bedtime story by hard. He murmured words while drooling, going to sleep in the tub. Sleepy sleepyhead. Now he is ready for bed. You scoop him out of the tub, dress him and continue the story.

There was a boy that could catch fish. There was not a fish he could not catch. He had a gift to catch fish. No challenge too great. The boy was wise. He knew his secret. In his dream a hot coal touch the tip of his tongue and he saw a path clearly. This path was narrow and steady. On the side of the path was a stream with fish. It was the duty of the fisherman to catch the fish. After catching the fish, it was given a choice to stay on the path or flop back into the water. Many stayed on the path. The child walks in his anointing.

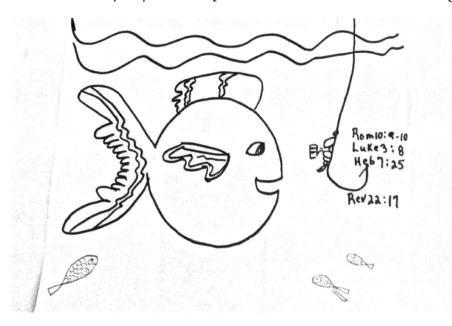

As mom finished the story, telling him one day he will catch the prize of a fish. And a grand fisherman of a man he will be. Life is good. All good thing comes from heaven.

THE END

P.S. We must tell our little ones. Our gift. Our children. We cannot afford to keep putting it off. They need to know they have a purpose, what that propose is. They are not a mistake. Tomorrow or more important now is not promise to us. We must prepare them in love for the end of the end days.

p.s. RFID!! Child dream of mark of the beast w/o no past knowledge/you tube

5 Dear Children tell of dream and vision/you tube/ Pokeman Go Leads 8 years old boy to hell

8-year-old goes to hell/you tube and many more;

My oldest child had a talk with me; it reminded me of one of my dark moments in my life. She was concern about a friend boy she had at school. She cares about him but he did not go to church. She wonders if he was faring well. She was about to act out in anger when she realizes that was being rebellious. That was her old ways. She said, "Mom if there any way you can find out something will you tell me?" I told her yes. I kept my doubts to myself. I knew this would happen; they've been away from schoolfriends for a while and she was happy with her friends.

Talking to the oldest child made me think back. It reminded me of moments in my life when I was spiraling out of control. My life was going through confusing scenarios, dramas, family problems, etc. One moment I was on top of the world and the next it felt like I do not know who I am. I went to sleep with drama, got through the day with drama. I even slept with drama or dreamed of drama. I had lost myself. I wanted no part of it but it was out of my control. This went on for a while.

I finally realized I was being spiritually attacked and wondered how it happens. I knew there will be trials and tribulations, but where is my breakthrough. I knew I was losing. I understood what it was about now. It felt like I was falling. I mean like the rug was being pulled from under my feet. Because you feel it, it's real, it's a real problem and it should not be happening to you. I made all the right choices in life, it should be roses now. I got the education. I am a good person. I make more than enough money to pay the bills, this car should not be giving me problems, my children - I don't know where to begin with that. I am active in the church and I pay my tithes. Life had been out of control for a while. It was still happening. I was still falling. So, tired there was days I wanted to hit the ground (end it, stop it). I had no control. I was still falling! Walking around on the edge! I was still walking around hoping to hit the ground, and I cannot get a balance in my life. Nothing feels like it is going right. The solution stood just out of my reach, almost there yet I never reach it.

When did I go from being one of the wise virgins to one of the foolish virgins?

I always wanted to live the life of a virtuous woman. When did I lose my balance, my purpose? When did I get lost again? I had accepted this imbalance as part of my life because I was falling for a long time. It felt like fate was teasing me. Just when I think I got it; I grab air. No answers there. I was barely holding on. Jesus did not forsake me and He did not let me be deceived.

A minister wisely put it in words when he said; we are prone to overestimate the benefits of things we desire and to underestimate the price involved such as losing our soul. Falling spiritually is definite a way the Lord cooled our enthusiasm in action we choose in life of this world. It does not mean we do not prosper. The Lord want us to be blessed and to prosper, but don't lose your way in Him. Don't walk away from Him.

The trial and tribulation of spiritual falling awakened me to my true position as a saint in the Lord. As I have told my children, you are fooling only yourself. In many cases the shoes fit my feet too well. I was a part time saint. I was forced to slow down and see that I am not the saints or true disciples of Jesus Christ. Praise God I realize this in time.

First the Lord will not have me ignorant. Which brings me to the old saying ignorance is bliss. Maybe for a moment and is it worth it. It like alcohol, when the buzz lifts the problem is still there. Truth comes in and cuts like a two-edge sword; because one reaps what one sow. I had to make a choice. Unfortunately, many of us take the path of least resistance (way of the world). Knowing or unknowing I am held accountable. I spiritually acted like a rebellious Jonah who played ignorant until he ended in the belly of the big fish. One would want to think amazing grace for Jonah, but his temperament of obedient did not last.

I have come to a spiritual halt; a spiritual awakens through the knowledge of Christ. This literally saved me. Truth set you free.

The confusion in my life narrowed my understanding causing unhealthy tunnel vision (all about me). I stayed on the board road and did not find the truth I seek. I did find imitations and thrill moments, but not truth. But I held on to faith, I believe the living word. There got to be a purpose to all of this; I have a right to be happy, to smile, to shine, and to live.

I developed spiritual sight and did not depend on my own understanding. But I kept the hope Praise be to God for his grace and mercy; it was then I saw the road I was on. Narrow or broad? I got off broad. I chose narrow because now I am listening to what the Spirit is saying to the church (that me). The Lord will not have me ignorant. He allowed me to see my path and were it will lead. Most of us will not be going to hell with our eyes close. We will know where we are going before we cease breathing.

I admire my daughter, she did not blindly take off as many were doing. She communicates and breathe. She trusts Jesus.

If the True Vine has touched you; you will know it. If you are connected to the True Vine you will know. If that person walking with you is in the True Vine, you will know. It is not meant to be a secret. So many secrets are sending people to hell. Skeletons in the closets need to be clean out.

Saints so many of us are expecting to stand and have taken a stand of neutrality, they are lukewarm. I mean elder of churches, pastors, church members in high and low positions. It's like Jesus being lead to the cross all over again. It's like Noah's days. It's like I thought I knew them but I did not. Jesus was rejected by his elders, his priests, his people thus his church. He was betrayed not only by Judas whom we know as the betrayal and the son of perdition, but his people repeatedly. I am not greater than my Lord. I have been betrayed by my church, by loves ones, and if it had not been by the power of the Holy Ghost I would have betrayed myself. In truth we are our own worst enemy besides the principalities of evil we fight in Jesus name. It hurts but we girdle up in the Word anyway. It hurt when I learn how to walk, but I kept walking. I will keep walking.

I do reap what I have sowed. All actions have consequences I learned. The actions may have felt good, but it does not mean the consequences will feel good. Only what you do for Christ will last and give life meaning. For example, break a commandment and it will come back to teach you a lesson. Whether you learned that lesson or not, is up to you. Remember Jonah.

For example, thou shalt not steal. You might have gotten away with it or so it seems. What the worse that could happen you party off that moment.

The wealth is like sand going through your fingers; you cannot stop it. You have sin, penalty for sin is death, you are spiritually dead. Secondly your belongings get stolen; or worst you can go jail or your body and soul die. You have experience what you put other through. Truth is you will reap what you have sow.

Sow blessings and love and reap it in abundance in Christ. We cannot beat Him in giving. If you do not change or die before it seems You have reaped your evil, that leave the spirit of that evil to fall from you to your bloodline if they do not find Christ.

What is the purpose of my life? Many would say live. That is a small part of it. Our purpose is to agape. We should love. Agape love! Love not connect with the world meaning (emotional) or sexual, but per the bible. Love ye one another as I have loved you. Love despite; we can do this through the direction and power of the Holy Ghost.

I can truly say I was not showing the love, I had my own bubble of entertainments going on. Lord forgive me.

I took time to sow a good seed, I did not know they were in vain. I could walk the walk and talk the talk and was miserable. Waiting for it to past. I always thought I am good person. I, I, I yes that was me I had to be deliver. It took me a while to get where I am now in the Lord. Thank the Lord for spiritually growth. Thank God for grace and mercy.

All good things come from heaven. I got married and had children. There were many bumps in my life and some mountains but Jesus gave me a way out through it all. One day most of my children grew up and I wonder who children are these. My children were taught that the living word and morals at home. I kept the faith; I kept praying. Prayers were answer because amazing grace the children turn out blessed. You have reaped what you sow.

I knew what I had to do. I wanted to be a virtuous woman; one of the wise virgin awaiting our Lord. I will start over. I prayed, Lord forgive me for my sins. Somehow, I have walked away from you forgive me Lord Jesus. I dedicate my life and my heart back to you.

I realized it was the little foxes and some big foxes that destroys my vine. It had disconnected me from the True Vine. I had let sin in. As the Lord began to minister to me, I realized I had grown impatience, which is not like me. I enjoyed a little gossip so a few white lies were okay. I now realized that I had become vain. What happen to my striving to be a virtuous woman? I bought and went place I should not have gone. I see that now. But I did not stay long. Now thinking about it; why did I go back? It was so nonchalant at the time. It felt so harmless. I am going to pray the prayer of faith and repent again.

I in vain increased my territory and not the Lord's territory. I learned as I increase his territory in my life my territory is blessed as I walk in the will of the Lord. I am blessed; time to build my integrity on truth.

A fact! I cannot serve two gods. Fact! Never build a house on sand. Fact! Jesus does saves. Fact! This earth which I am thankful for is not my permanent home.

I do have the love, joy, happiness in me through Jesus Christ. I have learned I must not lose sight of my way in Christ Jesus for only he knows the righteous path that will get me home. I went back to my notes and books to make certain I will never forget who I am in Christ. I will share them at the next meeting and with my children.

P.S. Now I add this prayer to my prayers.

> I repent for the remissions of my sins and ask for forgiveness. I ask Jesus to come into my life and heart. I ask by faith for salvation and to be made whole in Jesus name.

> In my time of need He was and will always be with me.

> In Jesus name, I build this house upon his Rock. Amen

Who am I say me?

I am the house!

I am the tabernacle not made by hand.

I am the church.

I am the bride of Christ.

I am the Kingdom of God.

I am the righteous of God in Christ.

I am a holy priest.

I am the light of the world.

I am a vessel that desire to be fitted for the Master's use.

I am born of God, and the evil one does not touch me.

I am one with the mind of Christ.

I am the peace of God that surpasses all understanding

I am a light that cannot be hid under a bushel.

I am a vessel that greater is He Who is in me than he in this world.

I am giving, and it is given to me; good measure, pressed down, shaken together, and running over, men give into my bosom.

I am one that has no lack for God supplies all my need per His riches and glory by Christ Jesus.

I am one that can do all things through Christ Jesus who strengthens me.

I am a vessel of God who shows forth the praises of God, who hath called me out of darkness and into His Marvelous Light.

I am joint-heir with Christ.

I am the temples of the Holy Spirit I am not my own.

I am as small as a grain of sand on a beach.

I am as big as a star of heaven that shines in the sky.

I am healed mentally, physically, spiritually, and thus completely by the stripes of Jesus Christ.

I am redeemed by the blood of the Lamb.

I am not conformed to this world, but transformed by the renewal of my mind by the living word.

I am of a chosen race, a royal priesthood, a holy nation, a people for his own possession, that I may proclaim the excellencies of Him who call me out of darkness into His marvelous light.

The house is blessed. Hebrew 3:6, Ephesians 2:21, 22. Wow I feel lighter, have you had moments when you were talking to yourself and turn out you were talking to the Lord. That right it just happens. Hallelujah!

WHAT IS THE BIBLE?

SOME SAY A HOLY BOOK
OLDER THAN TIME ITSELF.
IT HAS BEEN SAID TO BE A ROAD WAY
TO SHOW A PATH TO HEAVEN'S DOORS.
TO OTHERS IT'S A TREASURE MAP,
STREETS PAVED OF GOLD.
TO A DYING MAN IT CAN BE SAID
TO BE A PLACE OF LIFE ABUNDANTLY.
TO A WOMAN IN TURMOIL, HOLDING ON,
A PLACE OF PEACE, MANY HAVE KNOWN.
TO A PARENT IN DESPAIR WITH NO WHERE TO GO
THE WAY TO A PLACE WHERE TEARS WILL NEVER FLOW,
AND EVERYONE EVENTUALLY WILL WANT TO GO.
MANY DESIRE AND MAKE A START
BUT DEPART BEFORE THEY MAKE THE MARK,
TO SOME A CALM STILL VOICE
THAT HAS ALL THE ANSWERS.
THOUGH IT'S COMPOSED OF MANY WORDS
IT IS THE WORD.
TO A PARENT WHO HAVE LOST
THEIR CHILD TO THE STREET
HOPE FOR THE LOST SHEEP.
AN ARK OF SAFETY TO A DYING WORLD
SO, FROM THE HEART THESE TERMS HAVE EMBARK,
A LIVING WORD FROM A BOOK OF LIFE
STRENGTH AND GUIDANCE.
A RELIGIOUS MANUAL TELLING RIGHT FROM WRONG
BUT ONLY AS GOOD AS THE FAITH YOU HOLD ON.
WORDS OF GOD TO PERFORM AND LIVE BY,
LIFE ROAD MAP.
MY EVERYTHING PUTTING IT BOLDLY
INFALLIBLE WORD OF GOD.

RECORDING FOR DAILY LIVING,
UNCHANGING, UNRELENTING, EVERLASTING WORD FROM GOD.
A BOOK OF PROPHECY.
A BOOK OF ANCIENT STORIES HAPPENING TODAY.

TEACHES ABOUT LOVE, KINDNESS, AND LIFE
FULL OF GIFTS FROM GOD.
LONG SUFFERING FROM A SINLESS MAN
SHOWING THE RETURN OF THE PRODICAL SON.
LIFE DICTIONARY TO ENTERNAL LIFE
HOW TO HAVE A RELATIONSHIP WITH GOD.
A MYSTERY TO THOSE THAT DO NOT KNOW GOD.
JOY IN TIME OF SORROW,
DELIVERANCE AND HEALING WITH COMPLETE PEACE OF MIND.
THE WAY TEACHING, INSPIRE WORD OF GOD.
OPEN DOOR TO A SANTUARY OF PEACE,
LOTS OF LOVE LETTERS.
MY SWORD AND MY ARMOR
WITH INSTRUCTION ON HOW TO USE THE ABOVE.
THE TEN COMMANDMENT THAT WILL GET YOU HOME.
MY INSURANCE POLICY TO LIFE,
MY DAILY BREAD,
MY COMPANION,
HOLY WORD,
THE LAW,
MY MANUAL,
MY SURVIVAL KIT,
SENSE OF FULFILLMENT FOR THE INNER MAN.
MY GUIDE, MY INSPIRATION
LETTERS FROM JESUS CHRIST.
HOW TO BE SELFLESS AND HOW TO TREAT OTHER,
GUIDANCE FOR MEN TO DO THE RIGHT THINGS.
NOW YOU HAVE HEARD ABOUT THE WORD
HIDE IT IN YOUR HEART AND PLEASE ONLY GOD.
L. BRIDGES

I FALL ON BENDED KNEES

Every knee shall bow
Every tongue shall confess
Jesus is Lord; He is Lord of my life,
For this reason, I fall on bended knees.
Everything that hath breath praise ye the Lord
Submit to His will than truly live,
Lift holy hands and praise ye the Lord
For this reason, I fall on bended knees.
When I am stressed I give the Lord my best,
It is then, I confess
Lord I'm having a problem passing this test.
For this reason, I fall on bended knees.
I come before Him with a contrite heart.
I humble my being to my Lord.
My life is His; He has given me abundantly,
For this reason, I fall on bended knees.
He is the Potter I am but clay;
His hands shape me further,
He molds me into the way,
For this reason, I fall on bended knees.
As I descend in my flesh, Jesus ascends in my life.
I decrease daily as Jesus increases his Spirit in me
The flesh is weak but the Spirit is willingly
For this reason, I fall on bended knees.
I shall come to Him as a child.
My friend He will befriend,
My enemy He will bring an end.
For this reason, I fall on bended knees.
Lifted in pride is what sank the Titanic.
Humility would have kept it afloat
Stay under the blood
For this reason, I fall on bended knees
In the Lord, L. Bridges

Rumpelstiltskin

There was once was a man highly respected in the community. His quick wit and intelligence brought him fame and fortune from all over the land. Over the years there was a gradual change. He was right so often without humbleness that he began to upset his customers, later not only the customers but friends. As time changed and life produced other intelligence people, he did not adjust. He did not like sharing. He began to overthink problems and solutions because the simple answer was to simple. It became his way or no way. In other words, he was always right. The prestige decreased as his arrogance and pride increased. He was a selfish person. He began to lose the respect of his friends and customers. They tried to talk to him, but he was always right. While others were, wrong or misguided.

Once a fair man to look upon, he began to resemble the hardheaded, stiffness, and stubborn spirit in him. He began to resemble what had grown in his heart. His height decrease, his skin wrinkled, his legs became long and pole like. Thus, he picked up the name Rumpelstiltskin. People had begun to shun him because of his high minded, stiff necked and stubborn disposition.

An old college buddy, Fred, came to see Rumpelstiltskin. He heard about his recognition and was happy for him. He also heard about his depression. He wanted to cheer him up because this could not be the fun guy he knew from college.

Fred knocked on the door. Fred said, "hello, are you there?" The door swung open with force. When Fred saw Rumpelstiltskin, he could not believe his eyes. His friend had changed. He hardly recognized the man standing in front of him. Rumpelstiltskin did not seem to recognize him neither. Finally, Fred started joking about their college day and there it was. Recognition in Rumple eyes. For a moment there was a smile in his eyes but it did not last. Fred was persistent he did not let Rumple grumpiness run him off. He had prayed and hope his buddy could be reason with and improve.

He remembered days at college when his buddy would go off on trips, sometimes in the woods. He would not talk about it. Fred ask Rumple to go to church with him back then, but he always complained and said he did not have time. Fred asked Rumpelstiltskin, "where do you go to church now; I want to go with you. Fred asked, "Rumple". Rumpelstiltskin corrected him and said, "my name is Rumpelstiltskin and don't you forget it." Fred knew something dark had taken hold of his friend. He did not know what else to do but pray. Rumpelstiltskin wanted no part of that but Fred prayed anyway. He stayed as long as he could until Rumpelstiltskin put him out. Fred left sad and was sad.

Enough was enough. The people stop going to Rumpelstiltskin to do a job. They would rather go and pay extra to his competitors. There were those that tried to reach out to Rumpelstiltskin, but he rejected them, too. Rumpelstiltskin fame decreased and brought about his shame. He separated himself from people until he disappeared. Years went by and people forgot about Rumpelstiltskin. But Rumpelstiltskin did not forget about them. He felt he had a debt to repay the people that disrespected him. He decided to get his respect anyway he could. He became devious and more devious. He found painful ways for people to repay him. Rumpelstiltskin hit them where it hurt. The bargains did seem fair at first but would end with a cruel trick. He knew how to build up the need then drive the deal home. He came out on top of the deals.

Rumpelstiltskin had perfected his cruelty over the years. Rumpelstiltskin lived off his anger and cruelty, passed human years. Rumpelstiltskin lived alone and did a lot of traveling through the woods. Rumpelstiltskin became what he despised and looked like what he despises. He kept his ears on the alert to opportunities that would pass by. As he aged he realized his body would not last forever, he wanted to pass his legacy to a younger one of him. He wanted a minnie me. He did not want the knowledge he acquired through the years to go to waste. He did not think about a child until this time.

In a town, there lived a miller. The miller had to go before the King with a simple request, hoping to gain permission to expand his milling business. Upon coming to the castle and standing among people of high status, the miller felt inferior. When the miller went before the King he boasted. He introduced himself to the King and talked about his pride and joy, his daughter. The miller said, "my daughter is not just any daughter but one that is beautiful and talented. She could spin straw into gold." That got the bored King attention.

The King stopped the petitions right there. The King was always on the lookout to increase his holding in his kingdom. The King said, "I want to meet your daughter. Immediately!" The miller was speechless; he knew he had gone too far with his speech. He forced a grin and obeyed his King.

The daughter, being of an age to be a woman, could speak for herself. The daughter loved her father and knew his tongue got away from him at times. She did not want any harm to come to her father. When she saw his face, she knew something was wrong. She asked, "father what wrong this time?" When her father told her, what happen, he left nothing out. The miller knew he had put his daughter, his only daughter's life on the line. He wished it was his life. If he could he would change things. He did his fatherly duty and repented for the remission of his sin. He said, "forgive me daughter I acknowledged my tongue should have been bridle and I should have remembered the book of James." He asked, "Lord bridle my tongue and have mercy on my daughter."

The daughter being mature for her age comforted her father, she told him, "things will work out for our good. God will make a way."

The daughter packed a few things and her father took her to the castle. The King took the father at his word. He looked at the daughter took her to a small room fill with straw. There was a chair, spindle, and the room was filled with straws. The King escorted her into the small room. The King said, "I want all the straw in this room spin into gold or I will have your head." The King locked her in the room and left. She flopped down in the chair. She was amazed and said, "how rude;" she did not have time to explain her problem. She moans, "I am so lost."

Her mother's words came to mind. She began to cry. Her mother died when she was young. But she was taught how to pray. The quickest way to get her Father in heaven attention was to pray in Jesus name. Her mother told her many times "as the praises goes up the blessing come down." She prayed, "Lord have mercy on me, I need a miracle.

As she sat and sang about her problems to the Lord, low and behold it caught Rumpelstiltskin ears. He said, "that voice is beautiful." For a moment, just a moment he thought about passing her by. He knew the trouble he would bring. As he moved a step to go a force pull him back and before he knew it he was at her window.

The girl was startled when she saw the man. At first not recognizing what she was looking at. She remembered her manners and spoke to the man. She said, "good evening Sir." Before long she told him her woes and problems. He pretended to think on a solution, knowing that immediately his mind came up with an answer.

He said, "I think I can help. What will you give me for my work?" He looked at the necklace she was wearing. She kept stroking the necklace. Rumpelstiltskin knew it was important. He said, "I will take the necklace." They agreed upon the necklace she was wearing. The man came in through the bars of the window. Scoot the girl out of the way and begin to spin the straw into gold. By morning finished he was. The girl asleep on the floor did awaken when she heard the door open. She was as startled as the King when they saw the straw spun into gold.

She was given a meal but not release. When evening arrived, she was about to ask could she leave. The King announces, "it is time." The girl awaited and look at the King. Then the King looked back and she followed the King. He took her to another room. The room was bigger than the last one. Filled with straws! The King gave her the look. Yes, that looks. The King said firmly, "turn the straw into gold or I will have your head." He left locking the door behind him. The girl began to sing praises. She did not make arrangements with the strange man because she expected to go home. She did not know how to contact him. She felt she was on her own. By faith she began to pray and sing. She heard a knock on the bars. It was the man. They struck a deal on payment and upon completing the work he took her ring, the only ring jewelry her mom left her.

The King came and was very happy to see the room filled with gold. He made sure the girl was care for. The girl built herself up to speak. Then she commented gently, "I want to go home." The King told her, "if you spin this straw into gold one more night I will make you my wife."

The girl was ecstatic about becoming his wife. She wanted to live also. She thought to become a queen would be wonderful, but she knew she was not turning straw into gold. The King never asked how she did it; he kept increasing the task. She could imagine his thoughts; he enjoyed the increase in gold and thought it was wise to marry the goose that lays the golden egg. The woman wondered could she meet his expectations. She knew she was living on grace and mercy. She decided to let tomorrow account for itself. It was in the Lord hand anyway.

Eventually night came around and the King took the girl up into the tower. He took her to a BIGGER room filled with more STRAW. As soon as she went in with the King, he smiled at her and locked the door behind him. Knowing all will be well. The King happily thought, "she did this twice what the worst that can happen accept she need another night to finish." "I can allow that," said the King."

The girl saw, but not only is she up in a tower but the straw is triple in this room. She wondered, "how will this get done?" She was so caught up in her sorrow and crying she forgot to pray for strength, peace, and a way out. When there was a knock on her door and the man let himself in.

There was not a sympathetic bone in his body this night. He felt like his old self. He was ready to make the deal of a lifetime, a trade that they would talk about for generation to come. When the girl saw him, she cried harder because she had nothing to trade. The girl said, "I have no more jewelry; I am just a miller's daughter." But the man was a mastermind of wickedness and told her, do not to worry your mind about it now." Rumpelstiltskin said, "you are young; you have your whole life ahead of you." Then he said, "when the time come give me your first born." The girl desperate begin thinking like her father, use to living off loans, credit, and borrowed time thought nothing of this deal. She wondered what an unusually request. She believed when she became queen she would have something more valuable than her baby. Why he took her necklace and ring surely, he like jewelry. I worry about tomorrow when it gets here so she made the deal. She said, "alright it's a deal." The man hopped in the chair and went to spinning. The girl fell asleep when she heard the door opening then she awakened. The King stood amazed. He truly felt he was getting the best out of this deal. The room was packed with gold.

The King married the miller's daughter. The miller's daughter became Queen. The Queen on and off through she caught a glimpse of the imp-looking man. Just a glimpse, she convinced herself that shadow where playing tricks on her and all is well.

The imp-like man kept a close eye on the Queen because he wanted her child. The first born of the King and Queen, the man felt important. He knew the chaos and confusion he would cause in the land. Pain not only to the King and Queen, but to the country. He was thrilled and felt empowered that he had control, once again. He felt like a god. He jumped and dance.

The Queen became pregnant. She gave birth to a healthy child. Once the child was weaned she heard a knock on the child window. Her worse nightmare is now true. It was the imp-like man.

She felt all would be well. She would have something he wanted. Her jewelry now was more expensive than before. She opened the window to let him in, remembering she could not keep him out, she had no choice. She smiled and said, "greeting," and she tried to charm him. He pushed it all aside and strolled up to her. The imp-like man looked up into her face and said, "give me my child!" The Queen did not panic yet.

She offered the man many things in the kingdom. He firmly refused. He wanted the child. He told the Queen, "I am not getting any younger; you force me to be patient." "For a while I thought there would be no child," said imp-like man. When the Queen realize, all was lost, she began to cry. She began to twirl her hair, plait her hair, pull her hair and cried some more. The imp-like man puffed up. He felt in control like in the prime of his life. The deal of a lifetime; he felt good to make her cry. He wondered what do I have to lose. He said, "Queen I shall give you three days to guess my name. I will give you three guesses a day. Afterward I want my child." He strolled to the window with a quick look back and jump out the window.

(What do we do best when we are in over our head? We call out to the Father in Jesus name.) The Queen knew what it was like to be a mother and prayed, sing praises, and did shout out to the Lord. The Queen believed in miracles because she saw straw turn into gold, and she is a Queen who have been bless to have a child.

This was not a time to hold back, when the imp-like man came the first night. She tried common names. She said, "your name is Smith, Brown, or Jones." He laughed and climbed out the window. He told her he would be back.

The second night she tried to be more modern with the name. She asked the guards to give her popular names. They looked at her strange, but gave her common names. The guards wondered why she needs a name. The baby was born. Some thought she was expecting again. She was being smart and preparing names ahead of time.

The imp-like man came the second night. She guessed at the names. She said, "could it be George, James, or Bobby." This tickle the little man pink, he laughed so hard he tripped going out the door. He decided not to go far for tomorrow was the last night. This will be over.

The Queen was now furious, but she did not let anger overcome her. The Queen continued to sing praises, pray, and kept the faith, and the hope alive. Though she felt like running, and shouting she kept a calm countenance. She gave thanks to the Lord. Then it came to her, she called a huntsman and said, "follow the man that just left and listen to him closely; report to me anything he says." The huntsman replied, "yes my Queen."

The Queen renewed her vows to the Lord. She started paying her tithes. But most importantly she repented for the remission of her sins and renews her life with Christ. She started reading the living word to her child daily, those around her could not tell that a battle was raging, the kingdom was at peril. The Queen kept the faith.

As it became darker the huntsman thought he had lost the imp-like man. Then he realized the tracks were lighter. Then he lost those tracks, but he saw a light from a distance. He watched the stars because he was deep in the forbidden woods were many would not go. He followed the light. It was a camp fire. He heard laughter and saw dancing. The imp-like man was laughing and singing in riddles. He was tickle saying the same riddle over and over. The imp-like man said, "she would never guess my name for I am called R-U-M-P-E-L-S-T-I-L-T-S-K-I-N, that Rumpelstiltskin." The imp-like man laughs some more. The huntsman heard and started back to his Queen. He told her what he had heard.

The imp-like man let himself in and the Queen pretended to not know his name. Rumpelstiltskin turned around to get the child. Upon the third guess, she said, "your name is Rumpelstiltskin." Rumpelstiltskin was frozen in shocked. The shock quickly wore off, he began to stump his feet in anger. Rumpelstiltskin was so frustrated from his failure to obtain the child, he forgot his strength. He stumped so hard that the top part of his body twisted and went into his waist, he shrunk. He tried to pull himself out. He snatched hard. He ended up making himself into a knot and tearing himself in half. The Queen held the child and stood back; she did not know where this was going. He tried to hold himself together and started back stomping. He tried to drag himself to a door. He began to sink into the floor trying to get away with what he had. Rumpelstiltskin face true confusion for the first time. His other half sinking grab what was left and all of him went down and he was not heard of again in that kingdom.

The Queen kept her vow to the Lord. Though she was Queen and had a King she knew the Lord to be Lord of Lords and the King of Kings. He had proven to be her and their realm Prince of Peace and the kingdom prospers.

THE END

think I will go to town tomorrow. My hair is out of control. I have allowed my hair to go natural. It works better with certain products. I've got to get away from more of those products, maybe my mind will get stronger. I've strongly debating whether I should go. I went natural for this purpose, it supposed to be low maintenance. Hard to get away from all the chemicals, but I am close. I let go of cornbread so I can do this. One of those things that come through fasting and praying, I'll go early in the morning when it open and the customers and traffics will be slow.

I'm going to walk in faith and everything is going to be well. This have been a muggy day. Sarah Hair Store's prices have gone up. I saw what I needed, and got it. I added a few extra. Didn't want to call attention to myself. The cashier seemed friendly at the register. She asked, "is that all?" I smiled and say, "yes." She rung me up in no time and gave me the total. I took out my card and slide the chip in. She stopped smiling. She asked, "why do you not have the latest chip. Sometimes those cards do not go through." I was about to transformed on the lady when I realize who child I am. I say a silent pray for help and the screen said, "it is approved." She's surprised. She said, "my chip is using the latest tech etc. etc. etc." I ask her firmly, "are you trying to solicit me or sell me your products." She put the products in the bags. We smiled at each other and I am gone! My she acted like the chip was her pet pea (best friend).

I am going to be a true natural now, do not want to go through that again. For a moment I thought worst case scenario had happen so caught up in the moment was I. I've learned something.

I thought I saw a familiar face. He was one of the agent that came to my house. I think he saw me. I do not want to go through that again. I feel blessed to get away from their influences that first time. We are hearing from the internet that some third world countries are being force to receive the chip or die. Some are dying for what they believe in. To God be all glory. And there are nations that are accepting it as a tattoo or a latest cell phones.

Home sweet home! I brewed a cup of jasmine tea to get rid of this headache and get ready to can. The vegetables out of the garden did fair. For a moment I did not think they would produce. I prayed. I will talk to our herbalist about how to make natural hair products. With her knowledge on what available in the area; I can quickly learn how to do it myself. I do not want to go to town and get stress out. Not knowing if someone is about to grab me or give me a Judas' kiss and tell on me. I will keep the faith alive. If it God will that difference because that one appointment none of us will miss. I pray I am ready.

I woke up expecting something. What have I gotten myself into? Nothing that God cannot get me out of. I felt something was up, didn't expect it to be him or for him to find me so soon and to think I trusted him. Dreaming about snakes never goes well. I've canceled the dream in Jesus name. I've got my mind all work up I think of a new story to tell the children, that usually calm me. Got work to do. The children increase their reading. I wonder is it due to my stories. I will up my gain just in case. Be bless.

I Have Learned

I have learned in the worst-case situations, just don't get left behind.

I have learned, I'ld have missed the rapture.

This has not been my day. The only good thing is Jesus. Regardless! Until I learned I have walked away from Jesus. Somewhere in the crowd in my life of this world I let go of his hand. I let go of Jesus' hand.

I've been snap up, chew up, betrayed, served up on a tray, what had not happened. Did good, got evil in return. I must have been doing something right. I thought.

Then I learned I walk in my own reality. Made my world around me suit me. I did NOT line it up with the living word precept by precept.

I learned that I was not ready I did not even hear a trumpet. You've had one of those days. Don't expect sympathy. Times are tough, so get tough and get going.

I tried to tell one of my sisters in the Lord and was told there always someone worse off. Do good for evil. I haven't finished doing good yet.

That's right Paul said when I do good evil is present. Paul got a lot of good done. Then I will press on, knowing I need to get off by myself and let my spirit man loose.

Stop being on guard. Reinforce my armor. Settle my nerve.

HELP ME LORD! I must get back in touch with the power house. Must be empower. Too many negative situations are affecting me and not enough positive situations to cancel it. I tried to talk to a brother in the Lord. He told me you know you are human.

I ask him what do you mean by that. He just looked at me with pity.

I am having real issue and the house is on fire! Yea that's me. Not Holy Ghost Fire.

I need to be empower in touch with the power house. Purified by the power house. I need to make sure my equipment is working. Equipments – members should be working for Jesus.

When did I become so high maintenance? Oh yes, I spread myself to thin. Doing everything yet accomplish nothing. Get it started and dot here and there but complete nothing.

Fit! Form! Functionable! Not fitting. No form. Does not function through it have the appearance to function. Lord what is happening. (Now you know what time it is.)

Quiet time! Meditate time! Prayer time! Talk to the Lord's time! Upmost, listen to the Lord this time!

Benefits: **Peace**! I know what I should do. **Peace, truth**! There is nothing to do but obey God. **Peace, truth, joy**! Mind now unclutter and I can move forward. **Peace, truth, joy, love**! I can do all things through Christ Jesus our Lord. The world is under control because He has control. I do not exist like a dry leaf in the wind. I exist with purpose. I exist to be love. I exist as a spirit being in a physical.

I've learned.

I've learned when the spirit man is over ran by the physical man equal chaos.

Seem and unseen. Heard and unheard.

Conflict dissolves when lust of the flesh after the way of this world is brought to subjection to the Spirit of God.

I've learned.

Don't get left behind! Nothing is worth it. Not even your own life.

STAY TUNED FOR BOOK 2. WHERE IS THE LOVE?

Printed in the United States
By Bookmasters